Bradford Torrey

Spring Notes from Tennessee

Bradford Torrey

Spring Notes from Tennessee

ISBN/EAN: 9783337367374

Printed in Europe, USA, Canada, Australia, Japan

Cover: Foto ©Andreas Hilbeck / pixelio.de

More available books at **www.hansebooks.com**

SPRING NOTES FROM TENNESSEE

BY

BRADFORD TORREY

We travelled in the print of olden wars;
Yet all the land was green.
ROBERT LOUIS STEVENSON.

BOSTON AND NEW YORK
HOUGHTON, MIFFLIN AND COMPANY
The Riverside Press, Cambridge
1896

CONTENTS.

SPRING NOTES FROM TENNESSEE.

AN IDLER ON MISSIONARY RIDGE.

I REACHED Chattanooga on the evening of April 26th, in the midst of a rattling thunder-shower, — which, to look back upon it, seems to have been prophetic, — and the next morning, after an early breakfast, took an electric car for Missionary Ridge. Among my fellow - passengers were four Louisiana veterans fresh from their annual reunion at Birmingham, where, doubtless, their hearts had been kindled by much fervent oratory, as well as by much private talk of those bygone days when they did everything but die for the cause they loved. As the car mounted the Ridge, one of them called his companions' attention to a place down the valley where " the Rebels and the Yankees " (his own words) used to meet to play cards. " A regular gambling-hole," he called it. Their boys brought back lots

of coffee. In another direction was a spot
where the Rebels once " had a regular picnic," killing some extraordinary number of
Yankees in some incredibly brief time. I
interrupted the conversation, and at the
same time made myself known as a stranger and a Northerner, by inquiring after
the whereabouts of Orchard Knob, General
Grant's headquarters ; and the same man,
who seemed to be the spokesman of the
party, after pointing out the place, a savin-
sprinkled knoll between us and the city,
kindly invited me to go with him and his
comrades up to the tower, — on the site of
General Bragg's headquarters, — where he
would show me the whole battlefield and
tell me about the fight.

We left the car together for that purpose,
and walked up the slope to the foot of the
observatory, — an open structure of iron,
erected by the national government; but
just then my ear caught somewhere beyond
us the song of a Bachman's finch, — a song
I had heard a year before in the pine woods
of Florida, and, in my ignorance, was un-
prepared for here. I must see the bird and
make sure of its identity. It led me a little

chase, and when I had seen it I must look also at a summer tanager, a chat, and so on, one thing leading to another; and by the time I returned to the observatory the veterans had come down and were under some apple-trees, from one of which the spokesman was cutting a big walking-stick. He had stood under those trees — which were now in bloom — thirty years before, he said, with General Bragg himself.

I was sorry to have missed his story of the battle, and ashamed to have seemed ungrateful and rude, but I forget what apology I offered. At this distance it is hard to see how I could have got out of the affair with much dignity. I might have heard all about the battle from a man who was there, and instead I went off to listen to a sparrow singing in a bush. I thought, to be sure, that the men would be longer upon the observatory, and that I should still be in season. Probably that was my excuse, if I made one; and in all likelihood the veteran was too completely taken up with his own concerns to think twice about the vagaries of a stray Yankee, who seemed to be an odd stick, to say nothing worse of him. Well,

the loss, such as it was, was mine, not his;
and I have lost too much time in the way
of business to fret over a little lost (or
saved) in the way of pleasure. As for any
apparent lack of patriotic feeling, I suppose
that the noblest patriot in the world, if he
chanced to be also an ornithologist, would
notice a bird even amid the smoke of battle; and why should not I do as much on a
field from which the battle smoke had vanished thirty years before?

So I reason now; at the time I had no
leisure for such sophistries. Every moment
brought some fresh distraction. The long
hill — woodland, brambly pasture, and
shrubby dooryard — was a nest of singing
birds; and when at last I climbed the
tower, I came down again almost as suddenly as my Louisiana friends had done.
The landscape, — the city and its suburbs,
the river, the mountains, — all this would
be here to-morrow; just now there were
other things to look at. Here in the grass,
almost under my nose, were a pair of Bewick wrens, hopping and walking by turns,
as song sparrows may sometimes be found
doing; conscious through and through of

my presence, yet affecting to ignore it ; carrying themselves with an indescribable and pretty demureness, as if a nest were something never dreamed of by birds of their kind ; the female, nevertheless, having at that moment her beak bristling with straws, while the male, a proud young husband, hovered officiously about her with a continual sweetly possessive manner and an occasional burst of song. Till yesterday Bewick's wren had been nothing but a name to me. Then, somewhere after crossing the state line, the train stopped at a station, and suddenly through the open window came a song. " That 's a Bewick wren," I said to myself, as I stepped across the aisle to look out ; and there he stood, on the fence beside the track, his long tail striking the eye on the instant. He sang again, and once again, before the train started. Tennessee was beginning well with a visiting bird-gazer.

There must be some wrennish quality about the Bewick's song, it would seem : else how did I recognize it so promptly? And yet, so far as I am able to give an account of my own impressions, it had in my ears no resemblance to any wren song I had ever heard. I think it never suggested to me any music except the song sparrow's. The truth is, I suppose, that we *feel* resemblances and relationships of which the mind takes no cognizance.

I wandered at a venture down the further slope, turning this way and that as a song invited me. Here were Southerners and Northerners fraternally commingled: summer tanagers, Carolina wrens, blue-gray gnatcatchers, cardinal grosbeaks, chats, Bachman finches, field sparrows, chippers, white-throated sparrows, chewinks, indigo buntings, black-poll warblers, myrtle-birds, prairie warblers, a Maryland yellow-throat, a bay-breasted warbler, a black-and-white creeper, a redstart, brown thrushes, catbirds, a single mocking-bird, wood thrushes, red-eyed vireos, white-eyed vireos, wood pewees, a quail, and, in the air, purple martins and turkey buzzards. On the Ridge, as well as near the foot on our way up, a mocking-bird and a wood thrush sang within hearing of each other. Comparison as between birds so dissimilar is useless and out of place; but how shall a man avoid it? The mocking-bird is a great vocalist, — yes, and a great singer ; but to my Northern ears the wood thrush carried the day with his *voice*.

Having climbed the Ridge again, — though climbing might be thought rather too laborious a word for so gradual a slope, — and started down on the side toward the city, I came to a patch of blackberry vines, in the midst of which sat a thrasher on her nest, all a mother's anxiety in her staring yellow eyes. Close by her stood an olive-backed thrush. There, too, was my first hooded warbler, a female. She escaped me the next instant, though I made an eager chase, not knowing yet how common birds of her sort were to prove in that Chattanooga country.

In my delight at finding Missionary Ridge so happy a hunting-ground for an opera-glass naturalist, I went thither again the very next morning. This time some Virginia veterans were in the car (they all wore badges), and when we had left it, and were about separating, — after a bit of talk about the battle, of course, — one of them, with almost painful scrupulosity, insisted upon assuring me that if the thing were all to be done over again, he should do just as before.

One of his comrades, seeing me a Northerner, interrupted him more than once in a vain attempt to smooth matters over. They had buried the hatchet, he said; let bygones be bygones. But the first man was not to be cajoled with a phrase. He spoke without passion, with no raising of the voice, quite simply and amicably: he too accepted the result; the thing never *would* be done over again; only let his position be understood, — he had nothing to take back. It was impossible not to respect such conscientiousness. For my own part, at any rate, I felt no prompting to argue against it, being sufficiently " opinionated " to appreciate a difficulty which some obstinate people experience in altering their convictions as circumstances change, or accepting the failure of a cause as proof of its injustice. If a man is not *too* obstinate, to be sure, time and the course of events may bring him new light; but that is another matter. Once, when the men were talking among themselves, I overheard one say, as he pointed down the hill, " The Rebels were there, and the Union men yonder." That careless recurrence of the word " Rebel " came to me as a surprise.

The principal excitement of the morning was a glimpse of a Kentucky warbler, a bird most peculiarly desired. I had finished my jaunt, and was standing beside the bramble patch not far from the railway, where I had seen the hooded warbler the day before, when the splendid creature flashed into sight, saw me, uttered a volley of quick, clear notes, and vanished up the hillside. I ran after him, but might as well have remained where I was. "He *is* a beauty!" I find written in my notebook. And so he is, clothed in lustrous olive and the most gorgeous of yellows with trimmings of black, all in the best of taste, with nothing patchy, nothing fantastic or even fanciful. I was again impressed with the abundance of chats, indigobirds, and white-eyed vireos. Bachman sparrows were numerous, also, in appropriate localities, — dry and bushy, — and I noted a bluebird, a yellow-throated vireo, and, shouting from a dead treetop, a great crested flycatcher.

My most vivid recollection of this second visit, however, is of the power of the sun, an old enemy of mine, by whom, in my ignorance of spring weather in Tennessee, I allowed myself to be taken at a cruel noon-day disadvantage. Even now, in the deep frigidity of a Massachusetts winter, I cannot think of Missionary Ridge without seeing again those long stretches of burning sun-shine, wherein the least spot of shade was like a palm in the desert. In every such shelter I used to stand awhile, bareheaded; then, marking the next similar haven, so many rods ahead, I would hoist my umbrella and push forward, cringing at every step as if I were crossing a field under fire. Possibly I exaggerate, but, if I do, it is very little; and though it be an abuse of an exquisite poem, I say over to myself again and again a couplet of Miss Guiney's: —

" Weather on a sunny ridge,
    Showery weather, far from here."

In truth, early as the season was, the excessive heat, combined with a trying dog-day humidity, sadly circumscribed all my Tennessee rambles. As for my umbrella, my obligations to it were such that nothing but a dread of plagiarism has restrained me from entitling this sketch " An Umbrella on Missionary Ridge." Nature never intended me for a tropical explorer. Often I did nothing

more than seek a shady retreat and stay
there, letting the birds come to me, if they
would.

Improved after this indolent fashion, one
of the hottest of my forenoons became also
one of the most enjoyable. I left the car
midway up the Ridge, — at the angle of the
Y, — and, passing my thrasher's blackberry
tangle and descending a wooded slope, found
myself unexpectedly in a pleasant place, half
wood, half grassy field, through which ran a
tiny streamlet, the first one I had seen in
this dry and thirsty land. Near the streamlet, on the edge of the wood, quite by itself,
stood a cabin of most forlorn appearance,
with a garden patch under the window, —
if there *was* a window, as to which I do not
remember, and the chances seem against it,
— the whole closely and meanly surrounded
by a fence. In the door stood an aged white
woman, looking every whit as old and forlorn as the cabin, with a tall mastiff on one
side of her and a black cat on the other.

"Your dog and cat are good friends," I
remarked, feeling it polite to speak even to
a stranger in so lonesome a spot.

"Yes," she answered gruffly, "they 're

good friends, only once in a while he wants to kill her."

She said nothing more, and her manner did not encourage further attempts at neighborly intercourse; but as I passed the cabin now and then during the forenoon, the birds leading me about, I heard her muttering often and at considerable length to her hens and ducks. Evidently she enjoyed conversation as well as most people, only she liked to pick her own company. She was " Aunt Tilly," I learned afterwards, and had lived there by herself for many years; one of the characters of the city, a fortune-teller, whose professional services were in frequent request.

In this favored nook, especially along the watercourse, were many birds, some of them at home for the summer, but the greater part, no doubt, lying over for a day or two on their long northward journey. Not one of them but was interesting to me here in a new country, however familiar it might have become in New England. Here were at least eleven kinds of warblers: black-polls of both sexes, black-throated blues, chestnut-sides, myrtle-birds, golden warblers, black-

and - white creepers, redstarts (have we anything handsomer ?), Maryland yellow-throats, blue golden-wings, chats, and Ken. tuckies. Here were blue-gray gnatcatchers, bluebirds, wood thrushes, veeries, an olive-backed thrush, catbirds, thrashers, Carolina wrens, tufted titmice, a Carolina chickadee, summer tanagers uncounted, orchard orioles, field sparrows, chippers, a Bachman sparrow (unseen), a cardinal, a chewink, flocks of indigo-birds and goldfinches, red-eyed vireos, white-eyed vireos, a yellow-throated vireo, kingbirds, and a crested flycatcher.

In an oak at the corner of Aunt Tilly's cabin a pair of gnatcatchers had built a nest ; an exquisite piece of work, large and curi-ously cylindrical, — not tapering at the base, — set off with a profusion of gray lichens, and saddled upon one limb directly under another, as if for shelter. If the gnatcatcher is not a great singer (his voice is slender, like himself), he is near the head of his pro-fession as an architect and a builder. Twice, in the most senseless manner, one of the birds — the female, I had no doubt, in spite of the adjective just applied to her conduct — stood beside the nest and scolded at me ;

then, having freed her mind and attracted
my attention, she got inside and began peck-
ing here and there at the rim, apparently
giving it the final touches. The tufted tits
whistled unseen with all their characteristic
monotony. The veeries and the olive-back
kept silence, but the wood thrushes, as was
their daily habit, made the woods ring. One
of them was building a nest.

Most admired of all were the Kentucky
warblers, of which there were at least five.
It was my first real sight of them, and, fortunately, they were not in the least bashful.
They spent the time mostly on the ground,
in open, grassy places, especially about the
roots of trees and thorn-bushes, — the latter
now snowy with bloom, — once in a while
hopping a few inches up the bole, as if to
pick off insects. In movement and attitude
they made me think often of the Connecti-
cut warbler, although when startled they
took a higher perch. Once I saw one of
them under a pretty tuft of the showy blue
baptisia (*B. australis*), — a new bird in
the shadow of a new flower! Who says
that life is an old story? From the general
manner of the birds, — more easily felt than

defined, — as well as from their presence in
a group and their silence, I inferred, rightly
or wrongly, that they had but recently ar-
rived. For aught I yet knew, they might
be nothing but wayfarers, — a happy uncertainty which made them only the more interesting. Of their beauty I have already
spoken. It would be impossible to speak of
it too highly.

As I took the car at noon, I caught sight
of a wonderfully bright blood-red flower on
the bank above the track, and, as I was the
only passenger, the conductor kindly waited
for me to run up and pluck it. It turned
out to be a catchfly, and, like the Kentucky
warbler, it became common a little later.
" Indian pink," one of my Walden's Ridge
friends said it was called ; a pretty name,
but to me " battlefield pink " or "carnage
pink " would have seemed more appropriate.

I had found an aviary, I thought, this
open grove of Aunt Tilly's, with its treasure
of a brook, and at the earliest opportunity I
went that way again. Indeed, I went more
than once. But the birds were no longer
there. What I had seen was mainly a flock
of " transients," a migratory " wave." On

the farther side of the Ridge, however, I by
and by discovered a spot more permanently
attractive, — a little valley in the hillside.
Here was a spring, and from it, nearly dry
as it was, there still oozed a slender rill,
which trickled halfway down the slope
before losing itself in the sand, and here
and there dribbled into a basin commodious
enough for a small bird's bath. Several
times I idled away an hour or two in this
retreat, under the shadow of red maples,
sweet-gums, sycamores, and tupelos, making
an occasional sortie into the sun as an ad-
venturous mood came over me or a distant
bird-call proved an irresistible attraction.

They were pleasant hours, but I recall
them with a sense of waste and discomfort.
In familiar surroundings, such waitings
upon Nature's mood are profitable, whole-
some for body and soul; but in vacation
time, and away from home, with new paths
beckoning a man this way and that, and a
new bird, for aught he can tell, singing beyond the next hill,— at such a time, I think,
sitting still becomes a burden, and the cheerful practice of "a wise passiveness" a virtue
beyond the comfortable reach of ordinary

flesh and blood. Along the upper edge of the glen a road ran downward into the valley east of the Ridge, and now and then a carriage or a horseman passed. It would have been good to follow them. All that valley country, as I surveyed it from the railway and the tower, had an air of invitingness : beautiful woods, with footpaths and unfrequented roads. In them I must have found birds, flowers, and many a delightful nook. If the Fates could have sent me one cool day !

Yet for all my complaining, I have lived few more enjoyable Sunday forenoons than one that I passed most inactively in this same hillside hollow. As I descended the bank to the spring, two or three goldfinches were singing (goldfinch voices go uncommonly well in chorus, and the birds seem to know it) ; a female tanager sat before me calling *clippity, clippity ;* a field sparrow, a mocking wren, and a catbird sang in as many different directions; and a pair of thrashers — whose nest could not be far away — flitted nervously about, uttering characteristic moaning whistles. If they felt half as badly as their behavior indicated, their case was tragical indeed; but at the moment, instead of pitying them, I fell to wondering just when it is that the thrasher *smacks* (all friends of his are familiar with his resounding imitation of a kiss), and when it is that he whistles. I have never made out, although I believe I know pretty well the states of mind thus expressed. The thrasher is to a peculiar degree a bird of passion; ecstatic in song, furious in anger, irresistibly pitiful in lamentation. How any man can rob a thrasher's nest with that heartbroken whistle in his ears is more than I can imagine.

Indigo-birds are here, of course. Their number is one of the marvels of this country, — though indeed the country seems made for them, as it is also for chats and white-eyed vireos. A bit farther down the valley, as I come to the maples and tupelos, with their grateful density of shade, a wood pewee sings, and then a wood thrush. At the same moment, an Acadian flycatcher, who is always here (his nest is building overhead, as, after a while, I discover), salutes me with a quick, spiteful note. "No trespassing," he says. Landowners are pretty much alike. I pass on, but not far, and beside a little thicket I take up my stand, and wait. It is pleasant here, and patience will be rewarded. Yes, there is a magnolia warbler, my second Tennessee specimen; a great beauty, but without that final perfection of good taste (simplicity) which distinguishes the Kentucky. I see him, and he is gone, and I am not to be drawn into a chase. Now I have a glimpse of a thrush; an olive-back, from what I can see, but I cannot be sure. Still I keep my place. A blue-gray gnatcatcher is drawling somewhere in the leafy treetops. Thence, too, a cuckoo fires off a lively fusillade of *kuks*, — a yellow-bill, by that token. Next a black-poll warbler shows himself, still far from home, though he has already traveled a long way northward; and then, in one of the basins of the stream (if we may call it a stream, in which there is no semblance of a current), a chat comes to wash himself. Now I see the thrush again; or rather, I hear him whistle, and by moving a step or two I get him with my eye. He *is* an olive-back, as his whistle of itself would prove; and presently he begins to sing, to my intense delight. Soon two others are in voice with him. Am I on Missionary Ridge or in the Crawford Notch? I stand motionless, and listen and listen, but my enjoyment is interrupted by a new pleasure. A warbler, evidently a female, from a certain quietness and plainness, and, as I take it, a blue-winged yellow, though I have never seen a female of that species (and only once a male — three days ago at Chickamauga), comes to the edge of the pool, and in another minute her mate is beside her. Him there is no mistaking. They fly away in a bit of lovers' quarrel, a favorite pastime with mated birds. And look! there is a scarlet tanager; the same gorgeous fellow, I suppose, that was here two days ago, and the only one I have seen in this lower country. What a beauty he is! One of the finest; handsomer, so I think, than the handsomest of his all-red cousins. Now he calls *chip-cherr*, and now he breaks into song. There he falls behind; his cousin's voice is less hoarse, and his style less labored and jerky.

Now straight before me, up a woody aisle, an olive-backed thrush stands in full view

and a perfect light, facing me and singing,
a lovely chorister. Looking at him, I catch
a flutter of yellow and black among the
leaves by the streamlet; a Kentucky warbler,
I suspect, but I dare not go forward to see,
for now the thrushes are in chorus again.
By and by he comes up from his bath, and
falls to dressing his feathers: not a Kentucky, after all, but a Canadian flycatcher,
my first one here. He, too, is an exquisite,
with fine colors finely laid on, and a most
becoming jet necklace. While I am admir-
ing him, a blue yellow-back begins to practice his scales — still a little blurred, and
needing practice, a critic might say — somewhere at my right among the hillside oaks;
another exquisite, a beauty among beauties.
I see him, though he is out of sight. And
what seems odd, at this very moment his
rival as a singer of the scale, the prairie warbler, breaks out on the other side of me.
Like the chat and the indigo-bird, he is
abundantly at home hereabout.

All this woodland music is set off by
spaces of silence, sweeter almost than the
music itself. Here is peace unbroken; here
is a delicious coolness, while the sun blazes

upon the dusty road above me. How amiable
a power is contrast — on its softer side! I
think of the eager, bloody, sweaty, raging
men, who once stormed up these slopes, killing and being killed. The birds know nothing of all that. It might have been thousands of years ago. The very trees have forgotten it. Two or three cows come feeding
down the glade, with the lazy tinkle of a bell.
And now my new friend, the blue-winged
yellow warbler, sings across the path (across
the aisle, I was going to say), but only two
or three times, and with only two insignificant lisping syllables. The chary soul! He
sings to the eye, I suppose. I go over to
look at him, and my sudden movement star-
tles the thrushes, who, finding themselves
again in the singers' gallery, cannot refrain
from another chorus. At the same moment
the Canadian warbler comes into sight again,
this time in a tupelo. The blue-wings are
found without difficulty; they have a call
like the black-and-white creeper's. A single
rough-winged swallow skims above the treetops. I have seen him here before, and one
or two others like him.

As I return to the bed of the valley, a

female cardinal grosbeak flutters suspiciously about a thicket of tall blackberry vines. Her nest should be there, I think, but a hasty look reveals nothing. Again I come upon the Canadian warbler. If there is only one here, he is often in my way. I sit down upon the leaning, almost horizontal, bole of a large tupelo, — a new tree to me, but common in this country. The thick dark-colored bark is broken deeply into innumerable geometrical figures, giving the tree a noticeable, venerable appearance, as wrinkles lend distinction and character to an old man's face. Another species, which, as far as I can tell, should be our familiar tupelo of Massachusetts, is equally common, — a smaller tree, with larger leaves. The moisture here, slight as it now is, gives the place a vegetation of its own and a peculiar density of leafage. From one of the smaller tupelos (I repeat that word as often as I can, for the music of it) cross-vine streamers are swinging, full of red-and-yellow bells. Scattered thinly over the ground are yellow starflowers, the common houstonia, a pink phlox, and some unknown dark yellow blossom a little like the fall dandelion, — Cynthia, I guess.

My thoughts are recalled by a strong, sharp *chip* in a voice I do not recognize, — a Kentucky warbler's, as presently turns out. He walks about the ground amid the short, thin grass, seemingly in the most placid of moods; but at every few steps, for some inscrutable reason, he comes out with that quick, peremptory call. And all the while I keep saying to myself, "What a beauty!" But my forenoon is past. I rise to go, and at the motion he takes flight. Near the spring the goldfinches are still in full chorus, and just beyond them in the path is a mourning dove.

That was a good season: hymns without words, "a sermon not made with hands," and the world shut out. Three days afterward, fast as my vacation was running away, I went to the same place again. The olive-backed thrushes were still singing, to my surprise, and the Kentucky warblers were still feeding in the grass. The scarlet tanager sang (it is curious how much oftener I mention him than the comparatively unfamiliar, but here extremely common summer tanager), the cuckoo called, the Acadian flycatcher was building her nest, — on a horizontal limb of a maple, — and a goldfinch warbled as if he could never cease. A veery sang, also (I heard but one other in Tennessee), with a chestnut-sided warbler, two redstarts (one of them in the modest garb of his mother), a Carolina chickadee, a mocking wren, a pine warbler, a prairie warbler, and a catbird. In time, probably, all the birds for a mile around might have been heard or seen beside that scanty rill.

To-day, however, my mood was less Sundayish than before, and in spite of the heat I ventured across an open pasture, — where a Bachman's finch was singing an ingenious set of variations, and a rabbit stamped with a sudden loudness that made me jump, — and then through a piece of wood, till I came to another hollow like the one I had left, but without water, and therefore less thickly shaded. Here was the inevitable thicket of brambles (since I speak so much of chats and indigo-birds, the presence of a sufficiency of blackberry bushes may be taken for granted), and I waited to see what it would bring forth. A field sparrow sang from the hillside, — a sweet and modest tune that went straight to the heart, and had nothing to fear from a comparison with Bachman's finch or any other. What a contrast in this respect between him and his gentle-seeming but belligerent and tuneless cousin whom we call "chippy." [1] Here, likewise, were a pair of complaining Carolina wrens and an Acadian flycatcher. A thrush excited my curiosity, having the look of a gray-cheek, but showing a buff eye-ring; and while I was coaxing him to whistle, and so declare himself, — often a ready means of identification, and preferable on all accounts to shooting the bird, — there came a furious outburst from the depths of the brier patch, with a grand flurry of wings: a large bird and two smaller ones engaged in sudden battle, as well as I could make out. At the close of the *mêlée*, which ended as abruptly as it had begun, the thicket showed two wrens, a white-throated sparrow, and a female cardinal. The cardinal flew away; the affair was no business of hers, apparently; but in a minute she was back again, scolding. Then, while my back was turned, everything became quiet; and on my

---

[1] If I could have my way, he should be known as the doorstep sparrow. The name would fit him to a nicety.

stepping up to reconnoitre, there she sat in her nest with four eggs under her. At that moment a chat's loud voice was heard, and, turning quickly, I caught the fellow in the midst of a brilliant display of his clownish tricks, ridiculous, indescribable. At a little distance, it is hard to believe that it can be a bird, that dancing, shapeless thing, balancing itself in the air with dangling legs and prancing, swaying motions. Well, that is the chat's way. What more need be said? Every creature must express himself, and birds no less than other poets are entitled to an occasional " fine frenzy."

My little excursion had brought me nothing new, and, like all my similar ventures on Missionary Ridge, it ended in defeat. The sun was too much for me ; to use a word suggested by the place, it carried too many guns. I took a long and comfortable siesta under a magnificent chestnut oak. Then it was near noon, and, with my umbrella spread, I mounted the hill to the railway, and waited for a car.

LOOKOUT MOUNTAIN was at first a disappointment. I went home discouraged. The place was spoiled, I thought. About the fine inn were cheap cottages, — as if one had come to a second-class summer resort; while the lower slopes of the mountain, directly under Lookout Point on the side toward the city, were given up to a squalid negro settlement, and, of all things, a patent-medicine factory, — a shameful desecration, it seemed to me. I was half ready to say I would go there no more. The prospect was beautiful, — so much there was no denying; but the air was thick with smoke, and, what counted for ten times more, the eye itself was overclouded. A few northern warblers were chirping in the evergreens along the edge of the summit, between the inn and the Point, — black-polls and bay-breasts, with black-throated greens and Carolina wrens; and near them I saw with pleasure my first Tennessee phœbes. In the

street car, on the way back to Chattanooga,
I had for my fellow-passengers a group of
Confederate veterans from different parts of
the South, one of whom, a man with an
empty sleeve, was showing his comrades an
interesting war-time relic, — a bit of stone
bearing his own initials. He had cut them
in the rock while on duty at the Point thirty
years before, I heard him say, and now, remembering the spot, and finding them still
there, he had chipped them off to carry home.
These are all the memories I retain of my
first visit to a famous and romantic place
that I had long desired to see.

My second visit was little more remunera-
tive, and came to an untimely and inglorious
conclusion. Not far from the inn I noticed
what seemed to be the beginning of an old
mountain road. It would bring me to St.
Elmo, a passing cottager told me; and I
somehow had it fast in my mind that St.
Elmo was a particularly wild and attractive
woodland retreat somewhere in the valley, —
a place where a pleasure-seeking naturalist
would find himself happy for at least an
hour or two, if the mountain side should
insufficiently detain him. The road itself

looked uncommonly inviting, rough and deserted, with wild crags above and old forest below ; and without a second thought I took it, idling downward as slowly as possible, minding the birds and plants, or sitting for a while, as one shady stone after another offered coolness and a seat, to enjoy the silence and the prospect. Be as lazy as I could, however, the road soon gave signs of coming to an end ; for Lookout Mountain, although it covers much territory and presents a mountainous front, is of a very modest elevation. And at the end of the way there was no sylvan retreat, but a village ; yes, the same dusty little suburb that I had passed, and looked away from, on my way up. *That* was St. Elmo ! — and, with my luncheon still in my pocket, I boarded the first car for the city. One consolation remained : I had lived a pleasant hour, and the mountain road had made three additions to my local ornithology, — a magnolia warbler, a Blackburnian warbler, and a hairy woodpecker.

There was nothing for it but to laugh at myself, and try again ; but it was almost a week before I found the opportunity. Then

(May 7) I made a day of it on the mountain, mostly in the woods along the western bluffs. An oven-bird's song drew me in that direction, to begin with; and just as the singer had shown himself, and been rewarded with an entry as " No. 79 " in my Tennessee catalogue, a cuckoo, farther away, broke into a shuffling introductory measure that marked him at once as a black-bill. Till now I had seen yellow-bills only, and though the voice was perhaps a sufficient identification, a double certainty would be better, especially in the retrospect. Luckily it was a short chase, and there sat the bird, his snowy throat swelling as he cooed, while his red eye-ring and his abbreviated tail-spots gave him a clear title to count as " No. 80."

As I approached the precipitous western edge of the mountain, I heard, just below, the sharp, wiry voice of a Blackburnian warbler; a most splendid specimen, for in a moment more his orange-red throat shone like fire among the leaves. From farther down rose the hoarse notes of a black-throated blue warbler and two or three black-throated greens.

Here were comfortable, well-shaded boulders and delightful prospects, — a place to stay in ; but behind me stood a grove of small pine-trees, out of which came now and then a warbler's *chip ;* and in May, with everything on the move, and anything possible, invitations of that kind are not to be refused. Warbler species are many, and there is always another to hope for. I turned to the pines, therefore, as a matter of course, and was soon deeply engaged with a charming bevy of northward-bound passengers, — myrtle-birds, palm warblers, black-throated blues (of both sexes), a female Cape May warbler (the first of her sex that I had seen) magnolias, bay-breasts, and many black-polls. It makes a short story in the telling ; but it was long in the doing, and yielded more excitement than I dare try to describe. To and fro I went among the low trees (their lowness a most fortunate circumstance), slowly and with all quietness, putting my glass upon one bird after another as something stirred among the needles, and hoping every moment for some glorious surprise. In particular, I hoped for a cerulean warbler ; but this was not the cerulean's day, and, if I had but known it,

these were not the cerulean's trees. None
but enthusiasts in the same line will be able
to appreciate the delight of such innocent
" collecting," — birds in the memory instead
of specimens in a bag. Even on one's home
beat it quickens the blood ; how much more,
then, in a new field, where a man is almost a
stranger to himself, and rarities and novelties
seem but the order of the day. Again and
again, morning and afternoon, I traversed
the little wood, leaving it between whiles for
a rest under the big oaks on the edge of the
cliffs, whence, through green vistas, I gazed
upon the farms of Lookout Valley and
the mountains beyond. A scarlet tanager
called, — my second one here, — wood thrush
voices rang through the mountain side forest,
a single thrasher was doing his bravest from
the tip of a pine (our " brown mocking-
bird " is anything but a skulker when the
lyrical mood is on him), while wood pewees,
red-eyed vireos, yellow-throated vireos, black-
and-white creepers, and I do not remember
what else, joined in the chorus. Just after
noon an oven-bird gave out his famous aerial
warble. To an aspiring soul even a mountain top is but a perch, a place from which
to take wing.

All these birds, it will be noticed, were such as I might have seen in Massachusetts; and indeed, the general appearance of things about me was pleasantly homelike. Here was much of the pretty striped wintergreen, a special favorite of mine, with bird-foot violets, the common white saxifrage (dear to memory as the " Mayflower " of my childhood), the common wild geranium (cranesbill, which we were told was " good for canker "), and maple-leaved viburnum. One of the loveliest flowers was the pink oxalis, and one of the commonest was a pink phlox; but I was most pleased, perhaps, with the white stonecrop (*Sedum ternatum*), patches of which matted the ground, and just now were in full bloom. The familiar look of this plant was a puzzle to me. I cannot remember to have seen it often in gardens, and I am confident that I never found it before in a wild state except once. fifteen years ago, at the Great Falls of the Potomac. Yet here on Lookout Mountain it seemed almost as much an old friend as the saxifrage or the cranesbill.

I ate my luncheon on Sunset Rock, which literally overhangs the mountain side, and commands the finest of valley prospects ; and then, after another turn through the pines, where the warblers were still busy with their all-day meal, — but not the new warbler, for which I was still looking, — I crossed the summit and made the descent by the St. Elmo road, as before. How long I was on the way I am unable to tell ; I had learned the brevity of the road, and, like a schoolboy with his tart, I made the most of it. Midway down I caught sudden sight of an olive bird in the upper branch of a tree, with something black about the crown and the cheek. " What 's that ? " I exclaimed ; and on the instant the stranger flew across the road and up the steep mountain side. I pushed after him in hot haste, over the huge boulders, and there he stood on the ground, singing, — a Kentucky warbler. Seeing him so hastily, and on so high a perch, and missing his yellow under-parts, I had failed to recognize him. As it was, I now heard his song for the first time, and rejoiced to find it worthy of its beautiful author : *klurwée, klurwée, klurwée, klurwée, klurwée ;* a succession of clear, sonorous dissyllables, in a fuller voice than most warblers

possess, and with no flourish before or after.
Like the bird's dress, it was perfect in its
simplicity. I felt thankful, too, that I had
waited till now to hear it. Things should
be desired before they are enjoyed. It was
another case of the schoolboy and his tart;
and I went home good-humored. Lookout
Mountain was not wholly ruined, after all.

The next day found me there again, to
my own surprise, for I had promised myself
a trip down the river to Shellmound. In
all the street cars, as well as in the city
newspapers, this excursion was set forth as
supremely enjoyable, a luxury on no account
to be missed, — a fine commodious steamer,
and all the usual concomitants. The kind
people with whom I was sojourning, on Cameron Hill, hastened the family breakfast
that I might be in season; but on arriving
at the wharf I found no sign of the steamer,
and, after sundry attempts to ascertain the
condition of affairs, I learned that the
steamer did not run now. The river was
no longer high enough, it was explained; a
smaller boat would go, or might be expected
to go, some hours later. Little disposed to
hang about the landing for several hours,

and feeling no assurance that so doing would bring me any nearer to Shellmound, I made my way back to the Read House, and took a car for Lookout Mountain. In it I sat face to face with the same conspicuous placard, announcing an excursion for that day by the large and commodious steamer So-and-So, from such a wharf, at eight o'clock. But I then noticed that intending passengers were invited, in smaller type, to call at the office of the company, where doubtless it would be politely confided to them that the advertisement was a " back number." So the mistake was my own, after all, and, as the American habit is, I had been blaming the servants of the public unjustly.

I was no sooner on the summit than I hastened to the pine wood. At first it seemed to be empty, but after a little, hearing the drawling *kree, kree, kree,* of a black-throated blue, I followed it, and found the bird. Next a magnolia dropped into sight, and then a red-cheeked Cape May, the second one I had ever seen, after fifteen or twenty years of expectancy. He threaded a leafless branch back and forth on a level with my eyes. I was glad I had come.

Soon another showed himself, and presently it appeared that the wood, as men speak of such things, was full of them.   There were black-polls, also, with a Blackburnian, a bay-breast, and a good number of palm warblers, (typical *palmarum*, to judge from the pale tints); but especially there were Cape Mays, including at least two females.   As to the number of males it is impossible to speak; I never had more than two under my eye at once, but I came upon them continually, — they were always in motion, of course, being warblers, — till finally, as I put my glass on another one, I caught myself saying, in a tone of disappointment, "Only a Cape May."   But yesterday I might as well have spoken of a million dollars as "only a million."   So soon does novelty wear off. The magnolia and the Blackburnian were in high feather, and made a gorgeous pair as chance brought them side by side in the same tree.   They sang with much freedom; but the Cape Mays kept silence, to my deep regret, notwithstanding the philosophical remarks just now volunteered about the advantages derivable from a bird's gradual disclosure of himself.   Such pieces of wisdom, I have noticed, when by chance they do not fall into the second or third person, are commonly applied to the past rather than the present; a man's past being, in effect, not himself, but another. In morals, as in archery, the target should be set at a fair distance. The Cape May's song is next to nothing, — suggestive of the black-poll's, I am told, — but I would gladly have bought a ticket to hear it.

The place might have been made on purpose for the use to which it was now put. The pinery, surrounded by hard-wood forest, was like an island; and the warblers, for the most past, had no thought of leaving it. Had they been feeding in the hard wood, — miles of tall trees, — I should have lost them in short order. At the same time, the absence of undergrowth enabled me to move about with all quietness, so that none of them took the least alarm. Not a black-throated green was seen or heard, though yesterday they had been in force both among the pines and along the cliffs. A flock of myrtle warblers were surprisingly late, it seemed to me; but it was my last sight of them.

The reader will perceive that I was not exploring Lookout Mountain, and am in no position to set forth its beauties. It is eighty odd miles long, we are told, and in some places more than a dozen miles wide. I visited nothing but the northern point, the Tennessee end, the larger part of the mountain being in Georgia ; and even while there I looked twice at the birds, and once at the mountain itself.

At noon, I lay for a long time upon a flat boulder under the tall oaks of the western bluff, looking down upon the lower woods, now in tender new leaf and most exquisitely colored. There are few fairer sights than a wooded mountain side seen from above ; only one must not be too far above, and the forest should be mainly deciduous. The very thought brings before my eyes the long, green slopes of Mount Mansfield as they show from the road near the summit, — beauty inexpressible and never to be forgotten ; and miles of autumn color on the sides of Kinsman, Cannon, and Lafayette, as I have enjoyed it by the hour, stretched in the September sunshine on the rocks of Bald Mountain. Perhaps the earth itself will never be fully enjoyed till we are somewhere above it. The Lookout woods, as I now saw them, were less magnificent in sweep, but hardly less beautiful. And below them was the valley bottom, — Lookout Valley, once the field of armies, now the abode of peaceful industry : acres of brown earth, newly sown, with no trace of greenness except the hedgerows along the brooks and on the banks of Lookout Creek. And beyond the valley was Raccoon Mountain, wooded throughout; and behind that, far away, the Cumberland range, blue with distance.

A phœbe came and perched at my elbow, dropping a curtsey with old-fashioned politeness by way of " How are you, sir ? " and a little afterward was calling earnestly from below. This is one of the characteristic birds of the mountain, and marks well the difference in latitude which even a slight elevation produces. I found it nowhere in the valley country, but it was common on Lookout and on Walden's Ridge. Then, behind me on the summit, another northern bird, the scarlet tanager, struck up a labored, rasping, breathless tune, hearty, but broken and forced. I say labored and breathless; but, happily, the singer was unaware of his infirmity (or can it be I was wrong?), and continued without interruption for at least half an hour. If he was uncomfortably short-breathed, he was very agreeably long-winded. Oven-birds sang at intervals throughout the day, and once I heard again the black-billed cuckoo. Yes, Hooker was right: Lookout Mountain is Northern, not Southern. But then, as if to show that it is not exactly Yankee land, in spite of oven-bird and black-bill, and notwithstanding all that Hooker and his men may have done, a cardinal took a long turn at whistling, and a Carolina wren came to his support with a *cheery, cheery.* A faraway crow was cawing somewhere down the valley, no very common sound hereabout; a red-eye, our great American missionary, was exhorting, of course; a black-poll, on his way to British America, whispered something, it was impossible to say what; and a squirrel barked. I lay so still that a black-and-white creeper took me for a part of the boulder, and alighted on the nearest tree-trunk. He goes round a bole just as he sings, in corkscrew fashion. Now and then I caught some of the louder phrases of a distant brown thrush, and once, when every one else fell silent, a catbird burst out spasmodically with a few halting, disjointed eccentricities, highly characteristic of a bird who can sing like a master when he will, but who seems oftener to enjoy talking to himself. Lizards rustled into sight with startling suddenness; and one big fellow disappeared so instantaneously — in "less than no time," as the Yankee phrase is — that I thought "quick as a lizard" might well enough become an adage. Here and there I remarked a chestnut-tree, the burs of last year still hanging; and chestnut oaks were among the largest and handsomest trees of the wood, as they were among the commonest. The temperature was perfect, — so says my penciled note. Let the confession not be overlooked, after all my railing at the fierce Tennessee sun. It made all the pleasure of the hour, too, that there were no troublesome insects. I had been in that country for ten days, the mercury had been much of the time above 90°, and I had not seen ten mosquitoes.

I left my boulder at last, though it would have been good to remain there till night, and wandered along the bluffs to the Point. Here it was apparent at once that the wind had shifted. For the first time I caught sight of lofty mountains in the northeast; the Great Smokies, I was told, and could well believe it. I sat down straightway and looked at them, and had I known how things would turn, I would have looked at them longer; for in all my three weeks' sojourn in Chattanooga, that was the only half-day in which the atmosphere was even approximately clear. It was unfortunate, but I consoled myself with the charm of the foreground, — a charm at once softened and heightened, with something of the magic of distance, by the very conditions that veiled the horizon and drew it closer about us.

It is truly a beautiful world that we see from Lookout Point: the city and its suburbs; the river with its broad meanderings, and, directly at our feet, its great Moccasin Bend; the near mountains, — Raccoon and Sand mountains beyond Lookout Valley, and Walden's Ridge across the river; and everywhere in the distance hills and high mountains, range beyond range, culminating in the Cumberland Mountains in one direction, and the Great Smokies in another. And as we look at the fair picture we think of what was done here, — of historic persons and historic deeds. At the foot of the cliffs on which we stand is White House plateau, the battlefield of Lookout Mountain. Chattanooga itself is spread out before us, with Orchard Knob, Cameron Hill, and the national cemetery. Yonder stretches the long line of Missionary Ridge, and farther south, recognizable by at least one of the government towers, is the battlefield of Chickamauga. Here, if anywhere, we may see places that war has made sacred.

The feeling of all this is better enjoyed after one has grown oblivious to the things which at first do so much to cheapen the mountain, — the hotels, the photographers' shanties, the placards, the hurrying tourists, and the general air of a place given over to showmen. Much of this seeming desecration is unavoidable, perhaps ; at all events, it is the part of wisdom to overlook it, as, fortunately, by the time of my third visit I was pretty well able to do. If that proves impossible, if the visitor is of too sensitive a temperament, — to call his weakness by no worse a name, — he can at least betake himself to the woods, and out of them see enough, as I did from my boulder, to repay him for all his trouble.

The battlefield, as has been said, lies at the base of the perpendicular cliffs which make the bold northern tip of the mountain, — Lookout Point. I must walk over it, though there is little to see, and after a final look at the magnificent panorama I descended the steps to the head of the "incline," or, as I should say, the cable road. The car dropped me at a sentry-box marked "Columbus" (it was easy to guess in what year it had been named), and thence I strolled across the plateau, — so called in the narratives of the battle, though it is far from level, — past the Craven house and Cloud Fort, to the western slope looking down into Lookout Valley, out of which the Union forces marched to the assault. The place was peaceful enough on that pleasant May afternoon. The air was full of music, and just below me were apple and peach orchards and a vineyard.

In such surroundings, half wild, half tame, I had hope of finding some strange bird ; it would be pleasant to associate him with a spot so famous. But the voices were all familiar : wood thrushes, Carolina wrens, bluebirds, summer tanagers, catbirds, a Maryland yellow-throat, vireos (red-eyes and white-eyes), goldfinches, a field sparrow (the dead could want no sweeter requiem than he was chanting, but the wood pewee should have been here also), indigo-birds, and chats. In one of the wildest and roughest places a Kentucky warbler started to sing, and I plunged downward among the rocks and bushes (here was maiden-hair fern, I remember), hoping to see him. It was only my second hearing of the song, and it would be prudent to verify my recollection ; but the music ceased, and I saw nothing. At the turn, where the land begins to decline westward, I came to a low, semicircular wall of earth. Here, doubtless, on that fateful November morning, when clouds covered the mountain sides, the Confederate troops meant to make a stand against the invader. Now a wilderness of young blue-green persimmon-trees had sprung up about it, as about the Craven house was a similar growth of sassafras. I had already noticed the extreme abundance of sassafras (shrubs rather than trees) in all this country, and especially on Missionary Ridge.

With my thoughts full of the past, while my senses kept watch of the present, I returned slowly to the " incline," where I had five minutes to wait for a downward car. It had been a good day, a day worth remembering; and just then there came to my ear the new voice for which I had been on the alert: a warbler's song, past all mistake, sharp, thin, vivacious, in perhaps eight syllables, — a song more like the redstart's than anything else I could think of. The singer was in a tall tree, but by the best of luck, seeing how short my time was, the opera-glass fell upon him almost of itself, — a hooded warbler: my first sight of him in full dress (he might have been rigged out for a masquerade, I thought), as it was my first hearing of his song. If it had been also my last hearing of it, I might have written that the hooded warbler, though a frequenter of low thickets, chooses a lofty perch to sing from. So easy is it to generalize; that is, to tell

more than we know. The fellow sang again
and again, and, to my great satisfaction,
a Kentucky joined him,— a much better
singer in all respects, and much more be-
comingly dressed; but I gave thanks for
both. Then the car stopped for me, and we
coasted to the base, where the customary
gang of negroes, heavily chained, were re-
pairing the highway, while the guard, a
white man, stood over them with a rifle. It
was a strange spectacle to my eyes, and suggested a considerable postponement of the
millennium ; but I was glad to see the men
at work.

Two days afterward (May 10), in spite of
" thunder in the morning " and one of the
safest of weather saws, I made my final excursion to Lookout, going at once to the
warblers' pines. There were few birds in
them. At all events, I found few ; but
there is no telling what might have happened,
if the third specimen that came under my
glass — after a black-poll and a bay-breast
— had not monopolized my attention till I
was driven to seek shelter. That was the
day when I needed a gun ; for I suppose it
must be confessed that even an opera-glass

observer, no matter how much in love he may be with his particular method of study, and no matter how determined he may be to stick to it, sees a time once in a great while when a bird in the hand would be so much better than two in the bush that his fingers fairly itch for something to shoot with. From what I know of one such man, I am sure it would be exaggerating their tenderness of heart to imagine observers of this kind incapable of taking a bird's life under any circumstances. In fact, it may be partly a distrust of their own self-restraint, under the provocations of curiosity, that makes them eschew the use of firearms altogether.

My mystery on the present occasion was a female warbler, — of so much I felt reasonably assured; but by what name to call her, that was a riddle. Her upper parts were "not olive, but of a neutral bluish gray," with light wing-bars, "not conspicuous, but distinct," while her lower parts were "dirty, but unstreaked." What at once impressed me was her "bareheaded appearance" (I am quoting my penciled memorandum), with a big eye and a light eye-ring, — like a ruby-crowned kinglet, for which, at the first glance, I mistook her. If my notes made mention of any dark streaks or spots underneath, I would pluck up courage and hazard a glorious guess, to be taken for what it might be worth. As it is, I leave guessing to men better qualified, for whose possible edification or amusement I have set down these particulars.

While I was pursuing the stranger, but not till I had seen her again and again, and secured as many " points " as a longer ogling seemed likely to afford me, it began thundering ominously out of ugly clouds, and I edged toward some woodland cottages not far distant. Then the big drops fell, and I took to my heels, reaching a piazza just in time to escape a torrent against which pine-trees and umbrella combined would have been as nothing. The lady of the house and her three dogs received me most hospitably, and as the rain lasted for some time we had a pleasant conversation (I can speak for one, at least) about dogs in general and particular (a common interest is the soul of talk); in illustration and furtherance of which the spaniel of the party, somewhat against his

will, was induced to "sit up like a gentleman," while I boasted modestly of another
spaniel, Antony by name, who could do
that and plenty of tricks beside, — a perfect
wonder of a dog, in short. Thus happily
launched, we went on to discuss the climate
of Tennessee (whatever may be the soul of
talk, the weather supplies it with members
and a bodily substance) and the charms of
Lookout Mountain. She lived there the
year round, she said (most of the cottagers
make the place a summer resort only), and
always found it pleasant. In winter it
was n't so cold there as down below ; at any
rate, it did n't feel so cold, — which is the
main thing, of course. Sometimes when she
went to the city, it seemed as if she should
freeze, although she had n't thought of its
being cold before she left home. It is one
form of patriotism, I suppose, — parochial
patriotism, perhaps we may call it, — that
makes us stand up pretty stoutly for our
own dwelling-place before strangers, however we may grumble against it among ourselves. In the present instance, however,
no such qualifying explanation seemed necessary. In general, I was quite prepared to

believe that life on a mountain top, in a cottage in a grove, would be found every whit as agreeable as my hostess pictured it.

The rain slackened after a while, though it was long in ceasing altogether, and I went to the nearest railway station (Sunset Station, I believe) and waited half an hour for a train to the Point, chatting meanwhile with the young man in charge of the relic-counter. Then, at the Point, I waited again — this time to enjoy the prospect and see how the weather would turn — till a train passed on "the broad gauge" below. Just beyond Fort Cloud it ran into a fine old forest, and a sudden notion took me to go straight down through the woods and spend the rest of the day rambling in that direction. The weather had still a dubious aspect, but, with motive enough, some things can be trusted to Providence, and, the steepness of the descent accelerating my pace, I was soon on the sleepers, after which it was but a little way into the woods. Once there, I quickly forgot everything else at the sound of a new song. But *was* it new? It bore some resemblance to the ascending scale of the blue yellow-back, and might be the freak of some individual of that species. I stood still, and in another minute the singer came near and sang under my eye ; the very bird I had been hoping for, — a cerulean warbler in full dress; as Dr. Coues says, "a perfect little beauty." He continued in sight, feeding in rather low branches, — an exception to his usual habit, I have since found, — and sang many times over. His complaisance was a piece of high good fortune, for I saw no second specimen. The strain opens with two pairs of notes on the same pitch, and concludes with an upward run much like the blue yellow-back's, or perhaps midway between that and the prairie warbler's. So I heard it, I mean to say. But everything depends upon the ear. Audubon speaks of it as "extremely sweet and mellow" (the last a surprising word), while Mr. Ridgway is quoted as saying that the bird possesses "only the most feeble notes."

The woods of themselves were well worth a visit : extremely open, with broad barren spaces ; the trees tall, largely oak, — chestnut oak, especially, — but with chestnut. hickory, tupelo, and other trees intermingled. Here, as afterward on Walden's Ridge, I was struck with the almost total absence of mosses, and the dry, stony character of the soil, — a novel and not altogether pleasing feature in the eyes of a man accustomed to the mountain forests of New England, where mosses cover every boulder, stump, and fallen log, while the feet sink into sphagnum as into the softest of carpets.

Comfortable lounging-places continually invited me to linger, and at last I sat down under a chestnut oak, with a big broken-barked tupelo directly before me. Over the top of a neighboring boulder a lizard leaned in a praying attitude and gazed upon the intruder. Once in a while some loud-voiced tree-frog, as I suppose, uttered a grating cry. A blue-gray gnatcatcher was complaining, — snarling, I might have said; a red-eye, an indigo-bird, a field sparrow, and a Carolina wren took turns in singing; and a sudden chat threw himself into the air, quite unannounced, and, with ludicrous teetering motions, flew into the tupelo and eyed me saucily. A few minutes later, a single cicada (seventeen-year locust) followed him. With my glass I could see its monstrous red eyes and the orange edge of its wing. It kept silence; but without a moment's cessation the musical hum of distant millions like it filled the air, — a noise inconceivable.

I would gladly have sat longer, as I would gladly have gone much farther into the woods, for I had seen none more attractive; but a rumbling of thunder, a rapid blackening of the sky, and a recollection of the forenoon's deluge warned me to turn back. And now, for the first time, although I had been living within sound of locusts for a week or more, I suddenly came to trees in which they were congregated. The branches were full of them. Heard thus near, the sound was no longer melodious, but harsh and shrill.

It seemed cruel that my last day on Lookout Mountain should be so broken up, and so abruptly and unseasonably concluded, but so the Fates willed it. My retreat became a rout, and of the remainder of the road I remember only the hurry and the warmth, and two pleasant things, — a few wild roses, and the scent of a grapevine in bloom; two things so sweet and homelike that they could be caught and retained by a man on the run.

CHICKAMAUGA.

THE field of Chickamauga — a worthily resounding name for one of the great battle-fields of the world — lies a few miles south of the Tennessee and Georgia boundary, and is distant about an hour's ride by rail from Chattanooga. A single morning train outward, and a single evening train inward, made an all-day excursion necessary, and the time proved to be none too long. Unhappily, as I then thought, the sun was implacable, with the mercury in the nineties, though it was only the 3d of May; and as I was on foot, and the national reservation covers nine or ten square miles, I saw hardly more than a corner of the field. This would have been a more serious disappointment had my errand been of a topographical or historical nature. As the case was, being only a sentimental pilgrim, I ought perhaps to have welcomed the burning heat as a circumstance all in my favor; suiting the spirit of the place, and constraining me to a needful moderation. When a man goes in search of a mood, he must go neither too fast nor too far. As the Scripture saith, " Bodily exercise profiteth little." So much may readily be confessed now ; for wisdom comes with reflection, and it is no great matter to bear a last year's toothache.

From the railway station I followed, at a venture, a road that soon brought me to a comfortable, homelike house, with fine shade trees and an orchard. This was the Dyer estate, — so a tablet informed all comers. Here, in September, 1863, lived John Dyer, who suddenly found his few peaceful acres surrounded and overrun by a hundred thousand armed men, and himself drafted into service — if he needed drafting — as guide to the Confederate commander. Since then strange things had happened to the little farmhouse, which now was nothing less than a sort of government headquarters, as I rightly inferred from the general aspect of things round about, and the American flag flying above the roof. I passed the place without entering, halting only to smile at the antics of a white-breasted nuthatch, — my first Tennessee specimen, — which was hopping awkwardly about the yard. It was a question of something to eat, I suppose, or perhaps of a feather for the family nest, and precedents and appearances went for nothing. Two or three minutes afterward I came face to face with another apparition, a horseman as graceful and dignified, not to say majestic, as the nuthatch had been lumbering and ungainly; a man in civilian's dress, but visibly a soldier, with a pose and carriage that made shoulder-straps superfluous; a man to look at; every inch a major-general, at the very least; of whom, nevertheless, — the heat or something else giving me courage, — I ventured to inquire, from under my umbrella, if there were any way of seeing some of the more interesting portions of the battlefield without too much exposure to the sun. He showed a little surprise (military gentlemen always do, so far as I have observed, when strangers address them), but recovered himself, and answered almost with affability. Yes, he said, if I would take the first turn to the left, I should pass the spot over which Longstreet made the charge that decided the fate of the contest, and as he spoke he pointed out the field, which appeared to be part of the Dyer farm; then I should presently come within sight of the Kelly house, about which the fighting was of the hottest; and from there I should do well to go to the Snodgrass Hill tower and the Snodgrass house. To do as much as that would 'require little walking, and at the same time I should have seen a good share of what was best worth a visitor's notice. I thanked him, and followed his advice.

The left-hand road, of which my informant had spoken, ran between the forest — mostly of tall oaks and long-leaved pines — and the grassy Dyer field. Here it was possible to keep in the shade, and life was comparatively easy; so that I felt no stirrings of envious desire when two gentlemen, whom I recognized as having been among my fellow-passengers from Chattanooga, came up behind me in a carriage with a pair of horses and a driver. As they overtook me, and while I was wondering where they could have procured so luxurious a turnout, since I had discovered no sign of a public conveyance or a livery stable, the driver reined in his horses, and the older of the gentlemen put out his head to ask, " Were you in the battle, sir?" I answered in the negative; and he added, half apologetically, that he and his companion wished to get as many points as possible about the field. In the kindness of my heart, I told him that I was a stranger, like himself, but that the gentleman yonder, on horseback, seemed to be well acquainted with the place, and would no doubt answer all inquiries. With a queer look in his face, and some remark that I failed to catch, my interlocutor dropped back into his seat, and the carriage drove on. It was only afterward that I learned — on meeting him again — that he was no other than General Boynton, the man who is at the head of all things pertaining to Chickamauga and its history.

In the open field several Bachman finches were singing, while the woods were noisier, but less musical, with Maryland yellow-throats, black-poll warblers, tufted titmice, and two sorts of vireos. Sprinkled over the ground were the lovely spring beauty and the violet wood sorrel, with pentstemon, houstonia, and a cheerful pink phlox. Here I soon heard a second nuthatch, and fell into a kind of fever about its notes, which were clearer, less nasal, than those of our New

England birds, it seemed to me, and differently phrased. Such peculiarities might indicate a local race, I said to myself, with that predisposition to surprise which is one of the chief compensations of life away from home. As I went on, a wood pewee and a field sparrow began singing, — two birds whose voices might have been tuned on purpose for such a place. Of the petulant, snappish cry of an Acadian flycatcher not quite the same could be said. One of the "unreconstructed," I was tempted to call him.

The Kelly house, on the way to which through the woods my Yankee eyes were delighted with the sight of loose patches of rue anemones, was duly marked with a tablet, and proved to be a cabin of the most primitive type, standing in the usual bit of fenced land (the smallness of the houseyards, as contrasted with the miles of open country round about, is a noticeable feature of Southern landscapes), with a corn-house near by, and a tumble-down barn across the way. For some time I sat beside the road, under an oak; then, seeing two women, older and younger, inside the house, I asked leave to

enter, the doors being open, and was made
welcome with apparent heartiness. The
elderly woman soon confided to me that she
was seventy-six years old, — a marvelous
figure she seemed to consider it; and when
I tried to say something about her comparative youthfulness, and the much greater
age of some ladies of my acquaintance (no
names being mentioned, of course), she
would only repeat that she was awful old,
and should n't live much longer. She meant
to improve the time, however, — and the
unusual fortune of a visitor, — and fairly
ran over with talk. She did n't belong about
here. Oh no; she came from "'way up in
Tennessee, a hundred and sixty miles!"
"'Pears like I 'm a long way from home,"
she said, — "a hundred and sixty miles!"
Again I sought to comfort her. That was n't
so very far. What did she think of me,
who had come all the way from Massachusetts? She threw up her hands, and ejacu-
lated, "Oh, Lor'!" with a fervor to which
a regiment of exclamation points would
scarcely do justice. Yet she had but a
vague idea of where Massachusetts was, I
fancy; for pretty soon she asked, "Where

did you say you was from ? Pennsylvany ? ”
And when I said, “ Oh no, Massachusetts,
twice as far as that,” she could only repeat,
“ Oh, Lor’ ! ” Her grandson was at work
in the park, and she had come down to live
with him and his wife. But she should n’t
live long.

The wonder of this new world was still
strong upon her. “ Them moniment things
they ’ve put up,” she said, “ have you seen
’em ? Men cut in a rock ! — three of ’em ?
Have you seen ’em ? Ain’t they a sight to
see ? ” She referred to the granite monuments of the regulars, on which are life-size
figures in high relief. And had I seen the
tower on the hill, she proceeded to ask, — an
open iron structure, — and what did I think
of *that?* She would n’t go up in it for a
bushel of money. “ Oh yes, you would,” I
told her. “ You would like it, I ’m sure.”
But she stuck to her story. She would n’t
do it for a bushel of money. She should
be dizzy ; and she threw up her hands, literally, at the very thought, while her grand-
daughter sat and smiled at my waste of
breath. I asked if many visitors came here.
“ Oh, Lor’, yes ! ” the old lady answered.

"More 'n two dozen have been here from 'way up in Chicago."

The mention of visitors led the younger woman to produce a box of relics, and I paid her a dime for three minie-balls. "I always get a nickel," she said, when I inquired the price ; but when I selected two, and handed her a ten-cent piece, she insisted upon my taking another. Wholesale customers deserved handsome treatment. She had picked up such things herself before now, but her husband found most of them while grubbing in the woods.

The cabin was a one-room affair, of a sort common in that country ("cracker-boxes," one might call them, if punning were not so frowned upon), with a big fireplace, two opposite doors, two beds in diagonally opposite corners, and, I think, no window. Here was domestic life in something like its pristine simplicity, a philosopher might have said : the house still subordinate to the man, and the housekeeper not yet a slave to furniture and bric-à-brac. But even a philosopher would perhaps have tolerated a second room and a light of glass. As for myself, I remembered that I used to read of "poor white trash" in anti-slavery novels.

By this time the sun had so doubled its fury that I would not cross the bare Kelly field, and therefore did not go down to look at the " men cut in a rock ; " but after visiting a shell pyramid which marks the spot where Colonel King fell, — and near which I saw my first Tennessee flicker, — I turned back toward Snodgrass Hill, keeping to the woods as jealously as any soldier can have done on the days of the battle. At the foot of the hill was a well, with a rude bucket and a rope to draw with. Here I drank, — having to stand in the sun, I remember, — and then sat down in the shelter of large trees near by, with guideboards and index-fingers all about me, while a Bachman finch, who occupied a small brush-heap just beyond the well (*he* had no fear of sunshine), entertained me with music. He was a master. I had never heard his equal of his own kind, and seldom a bird of any kind, that seemed so much at home with his instrument. He sang " like half a dozen birds," to quote my own pencil ; now giving out a brief and simple strain, now running into protracted and intricate warbles ; and all with the most bewitching ardor and sweetness, and without the slightest suggestion of attempting to make a show. A field sparrow sang from the border of the grass land at the same moment. I wished he could have refrained. Nothing shall induce me to say a word against him; but there are times when one would rather be spared even the opportunity for a comparison.

As I went up the hill under the tall trees, largely yellow pines, a crested flycatcher stood at the tip of one of the tallest of them, screaming like a bird of war; and further on was a red-cockaded woodpecker, flitting restlessly from trunk to trunk, its flight marked with a musical woodpeckerish wing-beat, — like the downy's purr, but louder. I had never seen the bird before except in the pine-lands of Florida, nor did I see it afterward except on this same hill, at a second visit. It is a congener of the downy and the hairy, ranking between them in size, and by way of distinction wears a big white patch, an ear-muff, one might say, on the side of its head. Its habitat is strictly southern, so that its name, *Dryobates borealis*, though easily rememberable, seems but moderately felicitous.

Perhaps the most enjoyable part of the day — the most comfortable, certainly, but the words are not synonymous — was a two-hour siesta on the Snodgrass Hill tower, above the tops of the highest trees. The only two landmarks of which I knew the names were Missionary Ridge and Lookout Mountain; the latter running back for many miles into Georgia, like a long wooded plateau, till it rises into High Point at its southern end, and breaks off precipitously.

Farther to the south were low hills followed by a long mountain of beautiful shape, — Pigeon Mountain, I heard it called, — with elevations at each end and in the middle. And so my eye made the round of the horizon, hill after hill in picturesque confusion, till it returned to Missionary Ridge, with Walden's Ridge rising beyond, and Lookout Point on the left: a charming prospect, especially for its atmosphere and color. The hard woods, with dark pines everywhere among them to set them off, were just coming into leaf, with all those numberless, nameless, delicate shades of green that make the glory of the springtime. The open fields were not yet clear green, — if they

ever would be, — but green and brown intermixed, while the cultivated hillsides, especially on Missionary Ridge, were of a deep
rich reddish-brown. The air was full of
beautifying haze, and cumulus clouds in the
south and west threw motionless shadows
upon the mountain woods.

Around me, in different parts of the
battlefield, were eight or ten houses and
cabins, the nearest of them, almost at my
feet, being the Snodgrass house, famous as
the headquarters of General Thomas, the
hero of the fight, — the "Rock of Chickamauga," — who saved the Union army after
the field was lost. All was peaceful enough
there now, with the lines full of the week's
washing, which a woman under a volumi-
nous sunbonnet was at that moment taking
in (in that sun things would dry almost before the clothes-pins could be put on them,
I thought), while a red-gowned child, and a
hen with a brood of young chickens, kept
close about her feet. Her husband, like the
occupant of the Kelly house, was no doubt
one of the government laborers, who to-day
were burning refuse in the woods, — invisible fires, from each of which a thin cloud

of blue smoke rose among the trees. The Dyer house, in a direction nearly opposite the Snodgrass house, stood broadly in the open, with an orchard behind it, and dark savins posted here and there over the outlying pasture.

Even at noonday the air was full of music: first an incessant tinkle of cow-bells rising from all sides, wondrously sweet and soothing; then a continuous, far-away hum, like a sawmill just audible in the extreme distance, or the vibration of innumerable wires, miles remote, perhaps, — a noise which I knew neither how to describe nor how to guess the origin of, the work of seventeen-year locusts, I afterward learned; and then, sung to this invariable instrumental accompaniment, — this natural pedal point, if I may call it so, — the songs of birds.

The singers were of a quiet and unpretentious sort, as befitted the hour: a summer tanager; a red-eyed vireo; a tufted titmouse; a Maryland yellow-throat, who cried, " What a pity! What a pity! What a pity!" but not as if he felt in the least distressed about it; a yellow-throated vireo, full-voiced and passionless; a field sparrow, pretty far off;

a wood pewee; a yellow-billed cuckoo; a quail; a Carolina wren, with his "Cherry, cherry, cherry!" and a Carolina chickadee, —a modest woodland chorus, interrupted now by the jubilant cackling of a hen at the Snodgrass house (if a man's daily achievements only gave him equal satisfaction!) and now by the scream of a crested flycatcher.

The most interesting member of the choir, though one of the poorest of them all as a singer, is not included in the foregoing enumeration. While I lay dreaming on the iron floor of the tower, enjoying the breeze, the landscape, the music, and, more than all, the place, I was suddenly brought wide awake by a hoarse drawling note out of the upper branches of a tall oak a little below my level. I caught a glimpse of the bird, having run down to a lower story of the tower for that purpose. Then he disappeared, but after a while, from the same tree, he called again; and again I saw him, but not well. Another long absence, and once more, still in the same tree, he sang and showed himself: a blue-winged yellow warbler, an exquisite bunch of feathers, but with a song of the oddest and meanest, — two syllables, the first a mere nothing, and the second a husky drawl, in a voice like the blue golden-wing's. Insignificant and almost contemptible as it was, a shabby expression of connubial felicity, to say the least, I counted myself happy to have heard it, for novelty covers a multitude of sins.

The yellow-throated warblers were hardly less interesting than the blue-wing, though they threw me into less excitement. For a long time I heard them without heeding them. From the day of my arrival in Chattanooga I had been surrounded by indigo-birds in numbers beyond anything that a New England mind ever dreams of. As a matter of course they were singing here on Snodgrass Hill, or so I thought. But by and by, as the lazy notes were once more repeated, there came over me a sudden sense of difference. "*Was* that an indigo-bird?" I said to myself. "Was n't it a yellow-throated warbler?" I was sitting among the tops of the pine-trees; the birds had been droning almost in my very ears, and without a thought I had listened to them as indigo-birds. It confirmed what I had written in Florida, that the two songs are much alike; but it was a sharp lesson in caution. When a prudent man finds himself thus befooled, he begins to wonder how it may be with the remainder of that precious body of notions, inherited and acquired, to which, in all but his least complacent moods, he has been accustomed to give the name of knowledge.

Here was a lesson, also, in the close relation that everywhere subsists between the distribution of plants and the distribution of animals. These were the only yellow pines noticed in the neighborhood of Chattanooga; and in them, and nowhere else, I found two birds of the Southern pine-barrens, the red-cockaded woodpecker and the yellow-throated warbler.

At the base of the tower, when I finally descended, I paused a moment to look at a cluster of graves, eight or ten in all, unmarked save by a flagging of small stones; one of those family or neighborhood burying-grounds, the occupants of which — happier than most of us, who must lie in crowded cities of the dead — repose in decent privacy, surrounded by their own, with no ugly staring white slabs to publish their immemorable names to every passer-by.

From the hill it was but a few steps to the Snodgrass house, where a woman stood in the yard with a young girl, and answered all my inquiries with cheerful and easy politeness. None of the Snodgrass family now occupied the house, she said, though one of the daughters still lived just outside the reservation. The woman had heard her describe the terrible scenes on the days of the battle. The operating-table stood under this tree, and just there was a trench into which the amputated limbs were thrown. Yonder field, now grassy, was then planted with corn; and when the Federal troops were driven through it, they trod upon their own wounded, who begged piteously for water and assistance. A large tree in front of the house was famous, the woman said; and certainly it was well hacked. A picture of it had been in "The Century." General Thomas was said to have rested under it; but an officer who had been there not long before to set up a granite monument near the gate told her that General Thomas did n't rest under that tree, nor anywhere

else. Two things he did, past all dispute:
he saved the Federal army from destruction and made the Snodgrass farmhouse an
American shrine.

When our talk was ended I returned to
the hill, and thence sauntered through the
woods — the yellow-throated warblers singing all about me in the pine-tops — down to
the vicinity of the railroad. Here, finding
myself in the sun again, I made toward a
shop near the station, — shop and post-office
in one, — where fortunately there were such
edibles, semi-edibles, as are generally to be
looked for in country groceries. Meanwhile
there came on a Tennessee thunder shower,
lightning of the closest and rain by the
bucketful ; and, driven before it, an Indiana
soldier made his appearance, a wiry little
man of fifty or more. He had been spend-
ing the day on the field, he told me. In
one hand he carried a battered and rusty
cartridge-box, and out of his pockets he pro-
duced and laid on the counter a collection of
bullets. His were relics of the right stamp,
— found, not purchased, — and not without
a little shamefacedness I showed him my
three minie-balls. "Oh, you have got all

Federal bullets," he said ; and on my asking how he could tell that, he placed a Confederate ball beside them, and pointed out a difference in shape. He was a cheery, communicative body, good - humored but not jocose, excellent company in such an hour, though he had small fancy for the lightning, it seemed to me. Perhaps he had been under fire so often as to have lost all relish for excitement of that kind. He was not at the battle of Chickamauga, he said, but at Vicksburg ; and he gave me a vivid description of his work in the trenches, as well as of the surrender, and the happiness of the half-starved defenders of the city, who were at once fed by their captors.

All his talk showed a lively sense of the horrors of war. He had seen enough of fighting, he confessed ; but he could n't keep away from a battlefield, if he came anywhere near one. He had been to the national cemetery in Chattanooga, and agreed with me that it was a beautiful place ; but he had heard that Southern soldiers were lying in unmarked graves just outside the wall (a piece of misinformation, I have no doubt), and he did n't think it right or decent for the government to discriminate in that way. The Confederates were just as sincere as the Union men ; and anyhow, vengeance ought not to follow a man after he was dead. Evidently he had fought against an army and a cause, not against individuals.

When the rain was over, or substantially so, I proposed to improve an hour of coolness and freshness by paying another visit to headquarters ; but my Indiana veteran was not to be enticed out of shelter. It was still rather wet, he thought. " I 'm pretty careful of my body," he added, by way of settling the matter. It had been through so much, I suppose, that he esteemed it precious.

I set out alone, therefore, and this time went into the Dyer house, after drinking from a covered spring across the way. But there was little to see inside, and the three or four officers and clerks were occupied with maps and charts, — courteous, no doubt, but with official and counting-house courtesy ; men of whom you could well enough ask a definite question, but with whom it would be impossible to drift into random talk. There was far better company outside. Even while

I stood in the back door, on my way thither, there suddenly flashed upon me from a tree-top by the fence a splendid Baltimore oriole. He fairly "gave me a start," and I broke out to the young fellow beside me, " Why, there's a Baltimore oriole!" The exclamation was thrown away, but I did not mind.

It was the birds' own hour, — late afternoon, with sunshine after rain. The orchard and shade-trees were alive with wings, and the air was loud.   How brilliant a company it was a list of names will show: a mocking-bird, a thrasher, several catbirds, a pair of bluebirds, a pair of orchard orioles, a summer tanager, a wood pewee, and a flicker, with goldfinches and indigo-birds, and behind the orchard a Bachman finch. For bright colors and fine voices that was a chorus hard to beat.   As for the Baltimore oriole, the brightest bird of the lot, and the only one of his race that I found in all that country, he looked most uncommonly at home — to me — in the John Dyer trees. I was never gladder to see him.

A strange fate this that had befallen these Georgia farms, owned once by Dyer, Snod-grass, Kelly, Brotherton, and the rest: the plainest and most ordinary of country houses, in which lived the plainest of country people, with no dream of fame, or of much else, perhaps, beyond the day's work and the day's ration. Then comes Bragg retreating before Rosecrans, who is manœuvring him out of Tennessee. Here the Confederate leader turns upon his pursuers. Here he — or rather, one of his subordinates — wins a great victory, which nevertheless, as a Southern historian says, " sealed the fate of the Southern Confederacy." Now the farmers are gone, but their names remain ; and as long as the national government endures, pilgrims from far and near will come to walk over the historic acres. " This is the Dyer house," they will say, " and this is the Kelly house, and this is the Snodgrass house." So Fame catches up a chance favorite, and consigns the rest to oblivion.

My first visit to Chickamauga left so pleasant a taste that only two days afterward I repeated it. In particular I remembered my midday rest among the treetops, and my glimpse of the blue-winged warbler. It would be worth a day of my vacation to idle away another noon so agreeably, and hear again that ridiculous makeshift of a bird-song. Field ornithology has this for one of its distinguishing advantages, that every excursion leaves something for another to verify or finish.

This time I went straight to Snodgrass Hill through the woods, and was barely on the steps of the tower before I heard the blue-wing. As well as I could judge, the voice came from the same oak that the bird had occupied two days before. I was in luck, I thought; but the miserly fellow vouchsafed not another note, and I could not spend the forenoon hours in waiting for him. Two red-cockaded woodpeckers were playing among the trees, where, like the blue-wing and the yellow-throats, they were doubt-less established in summer quarters. "Sap-suckers," one of the workmen called them. They were common, he said, but likely enough he failed to discriminate between them and their two black-and-white relatives. Red-headed woodpeckers were *not* common here (I had seen a single bird, displaying its colors from a lofty dead pine), but were abundant and very destructive, so my informant declared, on Lookout Mountain.

Turkeys were still numerous on the mountain, and only the Sunday before one had been seen within the park limits.

The Bachman finch was again in tune at his brush-heap near the well, and between the music and a shady seat I was in no haste to go further. Finally, I experimented to see how near the fellow would let me approach, taking time enough not to startle him in the process. It was wonderful how he held his ground. The " Rock of Chickamauga " himself could not have been more obstinate. I had almost to tread on him before he would fly. He was a great singer, a genius, and a poet,

> " with modest looks,
> And clad in homely russet brown,"

and withal a lover of the sun, — a bird never to be forgotten. I wish I knew how to praise him.

To-day, as on my previous visit, I remarked a surprising scarcity of migrants. With the exception of black-poll warblers, I am not certain that I saw any, though I went nowhere else without finding them in good variety. Had my imagination been equal to such a stretch, I might have suspected that Northern birds did not feel at home on the scene of a great Southern victory. Here and there a nuthatch called, and again I seemed to perceive a decided strangeness in the voice. From the tip of a fruit-tree in the Kelly yard a thrasher or a mocker was singing like one possessed. It was impossible to be sure which it was, and the uncertainty pleased me so much, as a testimony to the thrasher's musical powers, that I would not go round the house in the sun to get a nearer observation. Instead, I went down to look at the monuments of the regulars, with their "men cut in a rock." Thence I returned to Snodgrass Hill for my noonday rest, stopping once more at the well, of course, and reading again some of the placards, the number of which just here bore impressive witness to the fierceness of the battle at this point. One inscription I took pains to copy : —

☞ Gen. J. B. Hood was wounded 11.10 a. m. 20 Sept. '63 in edge of timber on Cove Road ½ mile East of South, loosing his leg.

It was exactly eleven o'clock as I went up the hill toward the tower, and the workmen were already taking down their dinner-pails. Standard time, so called, is an unquestioned convenience, but the stomach of a day-laborer has little respect for convention, and is not to be appeased by a setting back of the clock. For my own part, I was not hungry, — in that respect, as in some others, I might have envied the day-laborers, — but as men of a certain amusing sort are said to turn up their trousers in New York when it rains in London, so I felt it patriotic to nibble at my luncheon as best I could, now that the clocks were striking twelve in Boston.

The hour (but it was two hours) calls for little description. The breeze was delicious, and the hazy landscape beautiful. The cow-bells and the locusts filled the air with music, the birds kept me company, and for half an hour or more I had human society that was even more agreeable. When the workmen had eaten their dinner at the foot of the tower, four of them climbed the stairs, and my field-glass proved so pleasing a novelty that they stayed till their time was up, to the very last minute. One after another took the glass, and no sooner had it gone the rounds once than it started again ; for meanwhile every man had thought of something else that he wanted to look at. They were above concealing their delight, or affecting any previous acquaintance with such a toy, and probably I never before gave so much pleasure by so easy a means. I believe I was as happy as if the blue-wing had sung a full hour. They were rough-looking men, perhaps, at least they were coarsely dressed, but none of them spoke a rude word ; and when the last moment came, one of them, in the simplest and gentlest manner, asked me to accept three relics (bullets) which he had picked up in the last day or two on the hill. It was no great thing, to be sure, but it was better : it was one of those little acts which, from their perfect and unexpected grace, can never be forgotten.

A jaunt through the woods past the Kelly house, after luncheon, brought me to a superfine, spick-and-span new road, — like the new government " boulevard " on Missionary Ridge, of which it may be a continuation, — following which I came to the Brotherton house, another war-time landmark, weather-beaten and fast going to ruin. In the woods — cleared of underbrush, and with little herbage — were scattered ground flowers: houstonia, yellow and violet oxalis, phlox, cranesbill, bird-foot violets, rue anemones, and spring beauties. I remarked especially a bit of bright gromwell, such as I had found first at Orchard Knob, and a single tuft of white American cowslip (*Dodecatheon*), the only specimen I had ever seen growing wild. The flower that pleased me most, however, was the blood-red catchfly, which I had seen first on Missionary Ridge. Nothing could have been more appropriate here on the bloody field of Chickamauga. Appealing to fancy instead of to fact, it nevertheless spoke of the battle almost as plainly as the hundreds of decapitated trees, here one and there one, which even the most careless observer could not fail to notice.

From the Brotherton house to the post-office was a sunny stretch, but under the protection of my umbrella I compassed it; and then, passing the Widow Glenn's (Rosecrans's headquarters), on the road to Crawfish Springs, I came to a diminutive

body of water, — a sink-hole, — which I
knew at once could be nothing but Bloody
Pond. At the time of the fight it contained
the only water to be had for a long distance.
It was fiercely contended for, therefore, and
men and horses drank from it greedily,
while other men and horses lay dead in it,
having dropped while drinking. Now a
fence runs through it, leaving an outer seg-
ment of it open to the road for the convenience of passing teams; and when I came in
sight of the spot, two boys were fishing
round the further edge. Not far beyond
was an unfinished granite tower, on which
no one was at work, though a derrick still
protruded from the top. It offered the best
of shade, — the shadow of a great rock, —
in the comfort of which I sat awhile, thinking of the past, and watching the peaceful
labors of two or three men who were culti-
vating a broad ploughed field directly before
me, crossing and recrossing it in the sun.
Then I took the road again; but by this
time I had relinquished all thought of walking to Crawfish Springs, and so did nothing
but idle along. Once, I remember, I turned
aside to explore a lane running up to a hill-

side cattle pasture, stopping by the way to
admire the activities — and they *were* activities — of a set of big scavenger beetles.
Next, I tried for half a mile a fine new road
leading across the park to the left, with
thick, uncleared woods on one side; and
then I went back to Bloody Pond.

The place was now deserted, and I took
a seat under a tree opposite. Prodigious
bullfrogs, big enough to have been growing
ever since the war, lay here and there upon
the water; now calling in the lustiest bass,
now falling silent again after one comical
expiring gulp. It was getting toward the
cool of the afternoon. Already the birds
felt it. A wood thrush's voice rang out
at intervals from somewhere beyond the
ploughed land, and a field sparrow chanted
nearer by. At the same time my eye was
upon a pair of kingbirds, — wayfarers hereabout, to judge from their behavior; a
crested flycatcher stood guard at the top of
a lofty dead tree, and a rough-winged swallow alighted on the margin of the pool, and
began bathing with great enjoyment. It
made me comfortable to look at him. By
and by two young fellows with fishing-poles
came down the railroad.

" Why is this called Bloody Pond ? " I asked.

" Why ? "

" Yes."

" Why, there were a lot of soldiers killed here in the war, and the pond got bloody."

The granite tower in the shadow of which I had rested awhile ago was General Wilder's monument, they said. His head-quarters were there. Then they passed on down the track out of sight, and all was silent once more, till a chickadee gave out his sweet and quiet song just behind me, and a second swallow dropped upon the water's edge. The pond was of the smallest and meanest, — muddy shore, muddy bottom, and muddy water; but men fought and died for it in those awful September days of heat and dust and thirst. There was no better place on the field, perhaps, in which to realize the horrors of the battle, and I was glad to have the chickadee's voice the last sound in my ears as I turned away.

ORCHARD KNOB AND THE NATIONAL CEMETERY.

THE street cars that run through the open valley country from Chattanooga to Missionary Ridge, pass between two places of peculiar interest to Northern visitors, — Orchard Knob on the left, and the national cemetery on the right. Of these, the Knob remains in all the desolation of war-time ; unfenced, and without so much as a tablet to inform the stranger where he is and what was done here ; a low, round-topped hill, dry, stony, thin-soiled, with out-cropping ledges and a sprinkling of stunted cedars and pines. Some remains of rifle-pits are its only monument, unless we reckon as such a cedar rather larger than its fellows, which must have been of some size thirty years ago, and now bears the marks of abundant hard usage.

The hill was taken by the Federal troops on the 23d of November, 1863, by way of "overture to the battle of Chattanooga," Grant, Thomas, Hooker, Granger, Howard,

and others overlooking the engagement from
the ramparts of Fort Wood. The next day,
as all the world knows, Hooker's men carried
Lookout Mountain, while the multitude below, hearing the commotion, wondered what
could be going on above them, till suddenly
the clouds lifted, and behold, the Confederates were in full flight. Then, says an eye-
witness, there "went up a mighty cheer from
the thirty thousand in the valley, that was
heard above the battle by their comrades on
the mountain." On the day following, for
events followed each other fast in that spec-
tacular campaign, Grant and Thomas had
established themselves on Orchard Knob,
and late in the afternoon the Union army,
exceeding its orders, stormed Missionary
Ridge, put the army of Bragg to sudden
rout, and completed one of the really deci-
sive victories of the war.

For a man who wishes to feel the memory
of that stirring time there is no better place
than Orchard Knob, where Grant stood and
anxiously watched the course of the battle,
a battle of which he declared that it was
won "under the most trying circumstances
presented during the war." For my own

part, I can see the man himself as I read the
words of one who was there with him. The
stormers of Missionary Ridge, as I have
said, after making the demonstration they
had been ordered to make, kept on up the
slope, thinking "the time had come to finish
the battle of Chickamauga." "As soon as
this movement was seen from Orchard
Knob," writes General Fullerton, "Grant
turned quickly to Thomas, who stood by his
side, and I heard him say angrily, 'Thomas,
who ordered those men up the ridge?'
Thomas replied in his usual slow, quiet manner, 'I don't know; I did not.' Then, ad-
dressing General Gordon Granger, he said,
'Did you order them up, Granger?' 'No,'
said Granger; 'they started up without
orders. When those fellows get started all
hell can't stop them.'" In the heat of battle
a soldier may be pardoned, I suppose, if his
speech smells of sulphur; and after the event
an army is hardly to be censured for beating
the enemy a day ahead of time. I speak as
a civilian. Military men, no doubt, find in-
subordination, even on the right side, a less
pardonable offense; a fact which may explain why General Grant, in his history of

the battle, written many years afterward,
makes no mention of this its most dramatic
incident, so that the reader of his narrative
would never divine but that everything had
been done according to the plans and orders
of the general in command.

Orders or no orders, the fight was won.
That was more than thirty years ago. It
was now a pleasant May afternoon, the
afternoon of May-day itself. The date, indeed, was the immediate occasion of my
presence. I had started from Chattanooga
with the intention of going once more to
Missionary Ridge, which just now offered
peculiar attractions to a stranger of ornithological proclivities. But the car was full
of laughing, smartly dressed colored people ;
they were bound for the same place, it appeared, on their annual picnic ; and, being
in a quiet mood, I took the hint and dropped
out by the way.

There was much to feel but little to see at
Orchard Knob ; and yet I recall two plants
that I found there for the first time ; a low
gromwell (*Lithospermum canescens*), with
clustered bright yellow flowers, and an odd
and homely greenish milkweed (*Asclepias*

obovata). The yarrow-leaved ragwort was there also, and the tall blue baptisia; but as well as I can recollect, not one dainty and modest nosegay-blossom; not even the houstonia, which seemed to grow everywhere, though after a strangely sparse and depauperate fashion. As I said to begin with, the Knob is a desolate place. It made me think of the Scriptural phrase about " the besom of destruction." I can imagine that mourners of the " Lost Cause," if such there still be, might see upon it the signs of a place accursed.

Far otherwise is it with the national cemetery. That is a spot of which the nation takes care. Here are shaven lawns, which, nevertheless, you are permitted to walk over; and shrubbery and trees, both in grateful profusion, but not planted so thickly as to make the inclosure either a wood or a garden; and where the ledge crops out, it is pleasingly and naturally draped with vines of the Virginia creeper. One thing I noticed upon the instant; there were no English sparrows inside the wall. The city is overrun with them beyond anything I have seen elsewhere; within two hundred feet of

the cemetery gate, as I passed out, there
were at least two hundred sparrows; but
inside, on three visits, I saw not one! How
this exemption had been brought about, I
did not learn; but it makes of the cemetery
a sort of heavenly place. I felt the silence
as the sweetest of music (it was a Sunday
afternoon), and thought instantly of Comus
and his "prisoned soul" lapped in Elysium.
If I knew whom to thank, I would name
him.

A mocking-bird, aloft upon the topmost
twig of a tall willow near the entrance, was
pouring forth a characteristic medley, in the
midst of which he suddenly called *wick-a-
wick*, *wick-a-wick*, in the flicker's very happi-
est style. "So flickers must now and then
come to Chattanooga." I said to myself, for
up to that time I had seen none. It was
a pleasure to hear this great songster of
the South singing above these thousands of
Northern graves. It seemed *right;* for time
and the event will prove, if, indeed, they
have not proved already, that the South,
even more than the North, has reason to be
glad of the victory which these deaths went
far to win.

A tablet on one of the cannons which stand upright on the highest knoll informs visitors that the cemetery was " established " in 1863. The number of burials is given as 12,876, of which nearly five thousand are of bodies unidentified. A great proportion of the stones bear nothing but a number. On others is a name, or part of a name, with the name of the State underneath. One I noticed that was inscribed : —

JOHN

N. Y.

An attendant of whom I inquired if any New England men were here, answered that there were a few members of the Thirty-third Massachusetts. I hope the New Englanders resident in Chattanooga do not forget them on Memorial Day.

Twice in the year, at least, the place has many Northern visitors. They arrive on wings, mostly by night, and such of them as came under my eye acted as if they appreciated the quiet of the inclosure, a quiet which their own presence made but the more appreciable. Scattered over the lawns were silent groups of white-throated sparrows, —

on their way to New Hampshire, perhaps, or it might be to upper Michigan ; and not far from the entrance, and almost directly under the mocking-bird, were two or three white-crowned sparrows, the only ones found in Tennessee. On an earlier visit (April 29) I saw here my only Tennessee robins — five birds ; and most welcome they were. Months afterward, a resident of Missionary Ridge wrote to me that a pair had nested in the cemetery that year, though to his great regret he did not know of it till too late. He had never seen a robin's nest, he added, and was acquainted with the bird only as a migrant. Such are some of the deprivations of life in eastern Tennessee. May and June without robins or song sparrows !

On the last of my three visits, a small flock of black-poll warblers were in the trees, and two of them gave me a pleasant little surprise by dropping to the ground, and feeding for a long time upon the lawn. That was something new for black-polls, so far as my observation had gone, and an encouraging thing to look at: another sign, where all signs are welcome, that the life of birds is less strictly instinctive — less a mat-

ter of inherited habit, and more a matter of
personal intelligence — than has commonly
been assumed. In general, no doubt, like
human beings, they do what their fathers
did, what they themselves have done here-
tofore. So much is to be expected, since
their faculties and desires remain the same,
and they have the same world to live in ;
but when exceptional circumstances arise,
their conduct becomes exceptional. In other
words, they do as a few of the quicker-
witted among men do — suit their conduct
to altered conditions. A month ago I should
have said, after years of acquaintance, that
no birds could be more strictly arboreal than
golden-crowned kinglets. But recently, I
happened upon a little group of them that
for a week or more fed persistently on the
ground in a certain piece of wood. Then
and there, for some reason, food was plenti-
ful on the snow and among the dead leaves ;
and the kinglets had no scruples about following where duty called them.

At the same time a friend of mine, a
young farmer, was at his winter's work in
the woods ; and being alone, and a lover of
birds, he had taken a fancy to experiment

with a few chickadees, to see how tame a little encouragement would make them. A flock of five came about him day after day, at luncheon-time, and by dint of sitting motionless he soon had two of them on terms of something like intimacy; so that they would alight on his hand and help themselves to a feast. He was not long in discovering, and reporting to me, that they carried much of the food to the trees round about, and packed it into crannies of the bark.

"Are you sure of that?" I asked.

"Oh, yes," he answered; "I saw them do it, and then I went to the trees and found the crumbs."

Did any one ever suspect the chickadee of such providence? If so, I never heard of it; and it is more likely, I think, that the birds had never before done anything of the sort; but now, finding suddenly a supply far in excess of the demand (one day they ate and carried away half a doughnut), they had sense enough to improve the opportunity. What they had done, or had not done, in times past, was nothing to the point, since they were creatures not of memory alone, but of intelligence and a measure of reason.

Beside the unmistakable migrants, —
white-throats, white-crowns, and black-polls,
— there were numbers of more southern
birds in the national cemetery. Among
them I noticed a yellow-billed cuckoo, crow
blackbirds, orchard orioles, summer tanagers,
catbirds, a thrasher, a bluebird, wood pewees,
chippers, blue-gray gnatcatchers, yellow warblers, wood thrushes, and chats. All these
looked sufficiently at home except the chats;
and it helps to mark the exceeding abundance of these last in the Chattanooga region
that they should show themselves without
reserve in a spot so frequented and so wanting in close cover. One of the orioles sang
in the manner of a fox sparrow, while one
that sang daily under my window, on Cameron Hill, never once suggested that bird,
but often the purple finch. The two facts
offer a good idea of this fine songster's quality and versatility. The organ tones of the
yellow-throated vireo and the minor whistle
of the wood pewee were sweetly in harmony
with the spirit of the place, a spirit hard
fully and exactly to express, a mingling of
regret and exultation. What mattered it
that all these men had perished, as it seemed,

before their time? — that so many of them
were lying in nameless graves? We shall
all die; few of us so worthily; and when
we are gone, of what use will be a name
upon a stone, a name which, after a few
years at the most, no passer-by will be concerned to read? Happy is he who dies to
some purpose. It would have been good, I
thought, to see over the cemetery gate the
brave old Latin sentence, *Dulce et decorum
est pro patria mori.*

The human visitors, of whom one day
there might have been a hundred, were
largely people of color. All were quiet
and orderly, in couples and family groups.
Most of them, I remarked, went to look at
the only striking monument in the grounds,
a locomotive and tender (the "General")
on a pedestal of marble — "Ohio's Trib-
ute to the Andrews Raiders, 1862." On
three faces of the pedestal are lists of the
"exchanged," the "executed," and the
"escaped."

One thing, one only, grated upon my feelings. In a corner of the inclosure is the
Superintendent's house, with a stable and
out-buildings; and at the gate the visitor is

suddenly struck in the face with this notice in flaring capitals: KEEP OUT! THIS MEANS YOU! That is brutality beyond excuse. But perhaps it answers its purpose. For my own part, I got out of the neighborhood as quickly as possible. I liked better the society of the graves; at such a price a dead soldier was better than a live superintendent; and to take the unpleasant taste out of my mouth I stopped to read again a stanza on one of the metal tablets set at intervals along the driveway: —

"On Fame's eternal camping ground
  Their silent tents are spread,
And Glory guards, with solemn round,
  The bivouac of the dead."

Far be the day when these Southern fields of Northern graves shall fall into forgetfulness and neglect.

AN AFTERNOON BY THE RIVER.

To an idler desirous of seeing wild life on easy terms Chattanooga offers this advantage, that electric cars take him quickly out of the city in different directions, and drop him in the woods. In this way, on an afternoon too sultry for extended travel on foot, I visited a wooded hillside on the further bank of the Tennessee, a few miles above the town.

The car was still turning street corner after street corner, making its zigzag course toward the bridge, when I noticed a rustic old gentleman at my side looking intently at the floor. Apparently he suspected something amiss. He was unused to the ways of electricity, I thought, — a verdancy by no means inexcusable. But as he leaned farther forward, and looked and listened with more and more absorption, the matter — not his ignorance, but his simple-hearted betrayal of it — began to seem amusing. For myself, to be sure, I knew nothing about electricity, but I had wit enough to sit still and let the car run; a degree of sophistication which passes pretty well as a substitute for wisdom in a world where men are distinguished from children not so much by more knowledge as by less curiosity. In the present instance, however, as the event proved, the dunce's cap belonged on the other head. My countryman's stare was less verdant than his next neighbor's smile; for in a few minutes the conductor was taking up a trap door at our feet, to get at the works, some part of which had fallen out of gear, though they were still running. Twice the car was stopped for a better examination into the difficulty, and at last a new wedge, or something else, was inserted, and we proceeded on our way, while the motorman who had done the job busied himself with removing from his coat, as best he could, the oil with which it had become besmeared in the course of the operation. It was rather hard, he thought, to have to spoil his clothes in repair-shop work of that kind, especially as he was paid nothing for it, and had to find himself. As for my rustic-looking seat-mate, he was an old hand at the business, it appeared, and his practiced ear had detected a jar in the machinery.

We left the car in company, he and I, at the end of the route, and pretty soon it transpired that he was an old Union soldier, of Massachusetts parentage, but born in Canada and a member of a Michigan regiment. Just how these autobiographical details came to be mentioned I fail now to remember, but in that country, where so much history had been made, it was hard to keep the past out of one's conversation. He had been in Sheridan's force when it stormed Missionary Ridge. As they went up the heights, he said, they were between two fires; as much in danger from Federal bullets as from Confederate; "but Sheridan kept right on." An old woman who lived on the Ridge told him that she asked General Bragg if the Yankees would take the hill. "Take the hill!" said Bragg; "they could as well fly." Just then she saw the blue-coats coming, and pointed them out to the General. He looked at them, put spurs to his horse, "and," added the woman, "I ain't seen him since." All of which, for aught I know, may be true.

The talkative veteran was now on his way
to find an old friend of his who lived somewhere around here, he did n't know just
where; and as my course lay in the same
general direction we went across lots and up
the hill together, he rehearsing the past,
and I gladly putting myself to school. In
my time history was studied from text-books;
but the lecture system is better. By and
by we approached a solitary cabin, on the
dilapidated piazza of which sat the very
man for whom my companion was looking.
"Very sick to-day," he said, in response
to a greeting. His appearance harmonized
with his words, — and with the piazza; and
his manners were pitched on the same key;
so that it was in a downright surly tone that
he pointed out a gate through which I could
make an exit toward the woods on the other
side of the house. I had asked the way,
and was glad to take it. Not that I was
greatly offended. A sick man on one of his
bad days has some excuse for a little impatience; a far better excuse than I should
have for alluding to the matter at this late
date, if I did not improve the occasion to
add that this was the only bit of anything

like incivility that I have ever received at
the South, where I have certainly not been
slow to ask questions of all sorts of people.

A little jaunt along a foot-path brought
me unexpectedly to a second cabin, unin-
habited. It was built of boards, not logs,
with the usual outside chimney at one end,
a broad veranda, a door, and no window; a
house to fill a social economist with admira-
tion at the low terms to which civilized life
can be reduced. Thoreau himself was out-
done, though the veranda, it must be confessed, seemed a dispensable bit of fashion-
able conformity, with forest trees on all
sides crowding the roof. Half the floor had
fallen away; yet the house could not have
been long unoccupied, for at one end the
wall was hung with newspapers, among
which was a Boston " weekly " less than two
years old. From it looked the portrait of a
New England college president, and at the
head of the page stood a list of "eminent
contributors." I ran the names over, but
somehow, in these wild and natural surroundings, they did not seem so very impressive. I think it has been said before, perhaps by Thoreau, that most of what we call

literature wears an artificial and unimportant look when taken out-of-doors.

Near this cabin I struck a road ("a sort of road," according to my note-book) through the woods, following which I shortly came to a grave-yard, or rather to a bunch of graves, for there was no inclosure, nor even a clearing. One grave — or it may have been a tiny family lot — was surrounded by a curb of stone. The others, with a single exception, were marked only by low mounds of gravel. The one exception was a grave with a head-board, — the grave of "Little Theodosia," a year and some months old. "Theodosia!" — even into a windowless cabin a baby brings romance. Under the name and the two dates was this legend: "She is happy." Of ten inscriptions on marble monuments nine will be found less simply appropriate.

By a circuitous course the wood road brought me to a larger cabin, in a larger clearing. Here a pleasant-spoken, neighborly woman, with a child in her arms, called off her dog, and pointed out a path beyond a pair of bars. That path, she said, would carry me to the river, — to the water's edge. And so it did, down a pleasant wooded hillside, which an unwonted profusion of bushes and ferns made exceptionally attractive. At the end of the path a lordly elm and a lordlier buttonwood, both of them loaded with lusty vines (besides clusters of mistletoe, I believe), gave me shelter from the sun while I sat and gazed at the strong eager current of the Tennessee hurrying onward without a ripple. As my foot touched the beach a duck — I could not tell of what kind — sprang out of the water and went dashing off. She had learned her lesson. In the duck's primer one of the first questions is : " What is a man ? " and the answer follows : " Man is a gun-bearing animal." In the treetops a golden warbler and a redstart were singing. Then I heard a puffing of steam, and by and by a tug came round a turn, pushing laboriously up stream a loaded barge. It was the Ocoee of Chattanooga, and the two or three mariners on board seemed to find the sight of a stranger in that unlooked-for place a welcome break in the monotony of their inland voyage.

On the bushy, ferny slope, as I returned,

two Kentucky warblers were singing in opposite directions. So I called them, at all
events. But they were too far away to be
gone after, as my mood then was, and soon
I began to wonder whether I might not be
mistaken. Possibly they were Carolina
wrens, whose *cherry* is not altogether unlike
the Kentucky's *klurwee*. The question
will perhaps seem unreasonable to readers
long familiar with the two birds; but let
them put themselves in a stranger's place,
remembering that this was only his third
or fourth hearing of the Kentucky's music.
As the doubt grew on me (and nothing
grows faster than doubt) I sat down and
listened. Yes, they were Kentuckies; but
anon the uncertainty came back, and I kept
my seat. Then a sound of humming-bird
wings interrupted my cogitations, and in
another moment the bird was before me,
sipping at a scarlet catchfly, — battlefield
pink. I caught the flash of his throat. It
was as red as the flower — beyond which
there is nothing to be said. Then he vanished (rather than went away), as humming-
birds do; but in ten minutes he was there
again. I was glad to see him. Birds of his

kind were rare about Chattanooga, though afterwards, in the forests of Walden's Ridge, they became as common as I ever saw them anywhere. The two invisible Kentuckies wore out my patience, but as I came to the bars another sang near me. Him, by good luck, I saw in the act, and for the time, at least, my doubts were quieted.

In the woods and thickets, as I sauntered along, I heard blue golden-winged warblers, two more Kentuckies, a blue-gray gnat-catcher, a Bachman's finch, a wood pewee, a quail, and the inevitable chats, indigo-birds, prairie warblers, and white-eyed vireos. Then, as I drew near the car track, I descended again to the river-bank and walked in the shade of lofty buttonwoods, willows, and white maples, with mistletoe perched in the upper branches, and poison ivy climbing far up the trunks; the whole standing in great contrast to the comparatively stunted growth, mainly oak, — and largely black jack, — on the dry soil of the hillside. Across the river were broad, level fields, brown with cultivation, in which men were at work, and from the same direction came loud rasping cries of batrachians of some

kind. For aught that my ear could detect,
they might be common toads uttering their
mysterious, discordant midsummer screams
in full chorus. Here were more indigo-birds,
with red-eyes, white-eyes, lisping black-poll
warblers, redstarts, a yellow-billed cuckoo
(furtive as ever, like a bird with an evil
conscience), catbirds, a thrasher, a veery in
song (a luxury in these parts), orchard orioles, goldfinches, and chippers. A bluebird
was gathering straws, and a carrion crow,
one of two seen in Tennessee, was soaring
high over the river.

The "pavilion," at the terminus of the
car route, was deserted, and I sat on the
piazza enjoying the really beautiful prospect
— the river, the woods, and the cultivated
fields. The land hereabout was all in the
market. In truth, the selling of building
lots seemed to be one of the principal in-
dustries of Chattanooga; and I was not
surprised to find the good-humored young
fellow behind the counter — with its usual
appetizing display of cigars, drinks, and
confectionery — full of the glories and im-
minent possibilities of this particular "suburb." He believed in the river. Folks

would come this way, where it was high and
cool. (On that particular afternoon, to be
sure, it was neither very high nor very
cool, but of course the weather is n't always
good anywhere.) "Lookout Mountain ain't
what it used to be," he said, in a burst of
confidence. "It's done seen its best days.
Yes, sir, it's done seen its best days." It
was not for a stranger, with no investment
in view, to take sides in such competitions
and rivalries. I believed in the river and
the mountain both, and hoped that both
would survive their present exploitation.
I liked his talk better when it turned upon
himself. Nothing is more exhilarating than
an honest bit of personal brag. He was
never sick, he told me. He knew nothing
of aches or pains. He could do anything
without getting tired. Save for his slavery
to the counter, he seemed almost as well off
as the birds.

A MORNING IN THE NORTH WOODS.

THE electric car left me near the Tennessee, — at "Riverview," — and thence I walked into the woods, meaning to make a circuit among the hills, and at my convenience board an inward-bound car somewhere between that point and the city. The weather was of the kind that birds love: warm and still, after heavy showers, with the sun now and then breaking through the clouds. The country was a suburb in its first estate: that is to say, a land company had laid out miles of streets, but as yet there were no houses, and the woods remained unharmed. That was a very comfortable stage of the business to a man on my errand. The roads gave the visitor convenience of access, — a ready means of moving about with his eyes in the air, — and at the same time, by making the place more open, they made it more birdy; for birds, even the greater part of wood birds, like the borders of a forest better than its darker recesses.

One thing I soon perceived: the rain had left the roads in a condition of unspeakable adhesiveness. The red clay balled up my heels as if it had been moist snow, till I pitched forward as I walked. I fancied that I understood pretty well the sensations of a young lady in high-heeled shoes. One moment, too, my feet were weighted with lead; then the mass fell off in a sudden big lump, and my next few steps were on air. A graceful, steady, self-possessed gait was out of the question. As for abstaining from all appearance of evil — well, as another and more comfortable Scripture says, "There is a time for everything." However, I was not disposed to complain. We read much about the tribulations of Northern soldiers on the march in Virginia, — of entire armies mud-bound and helpless. Henceforth I shall have some better idea of what such statements mean. In that part of the world, I am assured, rubber overshoes have to be tied on the feet with strings. Mother Earth does not believe in such effeminacies, and takes it upon herself to pull them off.

The seventeen-year locusts made the air

ring. Heard at the right distance, the
sound has a curious resemblance, noticed
again and again, to the far-away, barely
audible buzz of an electric car. For a week
the air of the valley woods had been full of
it. I wondered over it for a day or two,
with no suspicion of its origin. Then, as I
waited for a car at the base of Missionary
Ridge, a colored man who stood beside me
on the platform gave me, without meaning
it, a lesson in natural history.

" The locuses are goin' it, this mornin',
ain't they ? " he said.

" The locuses ? " I answered, in a tone of
inquiry.

" Yes. Don't you hear 'em ? "

He meant my mysterious universal hum,
it appeared. But even then I did not know
that he spoke of the big, red-eyed cicada
that I had picked off a fence a day or two
before and looked at for a moment with
ignorant curiosity. And even when, by
dint of using my own eyes, I learned so
much, I was still unaware that this cicada
was the famous seventeen-year locust. Here
in the north woods I more than once passed
near a swarm of the insects. At short range

the noise loses its musical character ; so that
it would be easy to hear it without divining
any connection between it and the grand
pervasive hum of the universal chorus.

One of the first birds at which I stopped
to look was a Kentucky warbler, walking
about the ground and pausing now and then
to sing; one of six or seven seen and heard
during the forenoon. Few birds are more
freely and easily observed. I mean in open
woodlands with clear margins, such as I was
now exploring. In a mountain forest, where
they haunt brookside jungles of laurel and
rhododendron, the story is different, as a
matter of course. How it happens that the
same bird is equally at home in surroundings
so dissimilar is a question I make no attempt
to answer.

All the hill woods, mostly oak, were dry
and stony ; but after a while I came unexpectedly to a valley, a place of another sort ;
not moist, to be sure, but looking as if it
had been moist at some time or other ; and
with pleasant grassy openings and another
set of trees — red maples, persimmons, and
sweet-gums. Here was a fine bunch of
birds, including many migrants, and I went

softly hither and thither, scanning the
branches of one tree after another, as a note
or the stirring of a leaf attracted me, ready
every minute for the sight of something
new and wonderful. I found nothing, —
nothing new and wonderful, I mean, — but I
had all the exhilaration of the chase. In the
company, nearly all of them in song, were
wood thrushes, a silent palm warbler (red-
poll), a magnolia warbler, three Canadian
flycatchers, many black-polls, one or two
redstarts, a chestnut-sided warbler, a black-
and-white creeper, a field sparrow, a yellow-
throated vireo, a wood pewee, an Acadian
flycatcher, and two or more yellow-billed
cuckoos. The red-poll was of a very pale
complexion (but I assert nothing as to its
exact identity, specific or sub-specific), and
seemed to me unreasonably late. It was
the 11th of May, and birds of its kind had
been passing through Massachusetts by the
middle of April. Chestnut-sides were scarce
enough to be interesting, and it was good
to hear this lover of berry fields and the
gray birch singing from a sweet-gum.

When at last I turned away from the
grassy glade, — where cattle were pasturing,

as I now remember, — and went back among
the dry hills (through the powdery soil of
which the almost daily showers seemed to
run as through a sieve), I presently caught
sight of a scarlet tanager,— a beauty, and,
except on the mountains, a rarity. Then I
stopped — on a street corner ! — to admire
the singing of a Bachman's finch, wishing
also to compare his plumage with that of a
bird seen and greatly enjoyed a few days
before at Chickamauga. To judge from
my limited observation, this is one of the
sparrows — the song sparrow being another
— which exhibit a strange diversity of individual coloration ; as if the fashion were
not yet fully set, or perhaps were being
outgrown. The bird here in the north
woods, so far as color and markings went,
might well enough have been of a different
species from that of the Chickamauga singer,
yet there was no reason to suspect the presence of more than one variety of *Peucæa*, so
far as I knew, and the music of the two
birds was precisely the same. A wonderfully sweet and various tune it is ; with
sometimes a highly ventriloquial effect, as if
the different measures or phrases came from

different points. It opens like the song
heard in the Florida flat-woods, but is even
more varied, both in voice and in musical
form. So it seemed to me, I mean to say;
but hearing the two a year apart, I cannot
speak without reserve. It is pleasanter —
as well as safer — to praise both singers than
to exalt one to the pulling down of the other.
In appearance, Bachman's finch is one of
the dullest, dingiest, least prepossessing
members of its great family; but its voice
and musical genius make it a treasure,
especially in this comparatively sparrowless
country of eastern Tennessee.

I have remarked that I found this bird
upon a street corner. Unhappily my notes
do not enable me to be more specific. It
may have been at the corner of Court and
Tremont Streets, or, possibly, at the junction
of Tremont and Dartmouth Streets. All
these names appear in my memoranda.
Boston people should have had a hand in
this business, I said to myself. It was on
Federal Street (so much I put down) that
I saw my only Tennessee rose-breasted grosbeak. He, or rather she, was the most
interesting bird of the forenoon, and matched

the one Baltimore oriole seen at Chickamauga. I heard the familiar *click*, as of
rusty shears, and straightway took chase.
For some minutes my search was in vain,
and once I feared I had been fooled. A bird
flew out of the right tree, as I thought, but
showed yellow, and the next moment set up
the *clippiticlip* call of the summer tanager.
Could that bird have also a note like the
rose-breast's? It was not impossible, of
course, for one does not exhaust the vocabulary of a bird in a month's acquaintance; but
I could not think it likely, thick as tanagers
had been about me; and soon the *click* was
repeated, and this time I put my eye on its
author, — a feminine rose-breast. Perhaps it
was nothing more than an accident that she
was my only specimen; but so showy a bird,
with so lovely a song and so distinctive a
signal, could hardly have escaped notice had
it been in any degree common.

Wood thrushes sang on all sides. They
had need to be abundant and free-hearted,
since they stand in that region for the whole
thrush family. Blue golden-winged warblers, too, were generously distributed, and,
as happens to me now and then in Massa-

chusetts, I found one with a song so absurdly
peculiar that I spent some time in making
sure of its author. It is to be hoped that
this tendency to individual variation will
persist ·and increase in the case of this species till something more melodious than its
present sibilant monotony is evolved; till
beauty and art are mated, as they ought to
be. Who would not love to hear the music
of all our birds a few millions of years
hence? What a singer the hermit thrush
will be, for example, when his tune is equal
to his voice! Indigo-birds, white-eyed vireos
and prairie warblers abounded. As for the
chats, they saluted me on the right and on
the left, till I said, " Chats, Chattanooga,"
and felt almost as if Nature had perpetrated
a huge fantastic pun on her own account.
If I could have had the ear of the enterprising owners of this embryo suburb, — a syn-
dicate, I dare say they call themselves, —
I would have suggested to them to name it
" Chat City."

I wandered carelessly about, now following
a bird over a rounded hill (one, I remember,
was covered literally from end to end with
the common brake, — *Pteris*, — which will

give the reader an idea of its sterility), now keeping to the road. In such a soil flowers were naturally scarce; but I noticed houstonia, phlox, hieracium, senecio, pentstemon, and specularia. Like the brake, the names are suggestive of barrenness. The senecio (ragwort), a species with finely cut leaves (*S. millefolium*), was first seen on Missionary Ridge. There, as here, it had a strange, misplaced appearance in my eyes, looking much like our familiar *S. aureus*, but growing in dry woods!

So the morning passed. The hours were far too brief, and I would have stretched them into the afternoon, but that my trunk was packed for Walden's Ridge. It was necessary to think of getting back to the city, and I took a quicker pace. Two more Kentucky warblers detained me for a moment; a quail sprang up from under my feet; and on the other side of the way an oven-bird sang — the only one found in the valley. Then I came to the car-track; but somehow things wore an unexpected look, and a preacher, very black, solemn, and shiny, gave me to understand, in answer to a question, that the city lay not where I thought, but in an opposite direction. Instead of making a circuit I had cut straight across the country (an unusual form of bewilderment), and had come to another railway. But no harm was done. In that corner of the world all roads lead to Chattanooga.

A WEEK ON WALDEN'S RIDGE.

I.

THROUGHOUT my stay in Chattanooga I looked often and with desire at a long, flat-topped, perpendicular-sided, densely wooded mountain, beyond the Tennessee River. Its name was Walden's Ridge, I was told; the top of it was eighty miles long and ten or twelve miles wide ; if I wanted a bit of wild country, that was the place for me. Was it accessible? I asked. And was there any reasonable way of living there? Oh yes; carriages ran every afternoon from the city, and there were several small hotels on the mountain. So it happened that I went to Walden's Ridge for my last week in Tennessee, and have ever since thanked my stars — as New England Christians used to say, in my boyhood — for giving me the good wine at the end of the feast.

The wine, it is true, was a little too freely watered. I went up the mountain in a rain, and came down again in a rain, and of the

seven intervening days five were showery.
The showers, mostly with thunder and
lightning, were of the sort that make an
umbrella ridiculous, and my jaunts, as a
rule, took me far from shelter. Yet I had
little to complain of. Now and then I was
put to my trumps, as it were ; my walk was
sometimes grievously abbreviated, and my
pace uncomfortably hurried, but by one
happy accident and another I always escaped
a drenching. Worse than the water that
fell — worse, and not to be escaped, even by
accident — was that which saturated the
atmosphere, making every day a dogday, and
the week a seven-day sweat. And then, as
if to even the account, on the last night of
my stay I was kept awake for hours shivering with cold ; and in the morning, after
putting on all the clothing I could wear,
and breakfasting in a snowstorm, I rode
down the mountain in a state suggestive of
approaching congelation. "My feet are
frozen, I know they are," said the lady who
sat beside me in the wagon ; but she was
mistaken.

This sudden drop in the temperature
seemed to be a trial even to the natives.

As we drove into Chattanooga, it was impossible not to smile at the pinched and woebegone appearance of the colored people. What had they to do with weather that makes a man hurry? And the next morning, when an enterprising, bright-faced white boy ran up to me with a "'Times,' sir? Have a 'Times'?" I fear he quite misapprehended the more or less quizzical expression which I am sure came into my face. I was looking at his black woolen mittens, and thinking how well he was mothered. It was the 19th of May; for at least three weeks, to my own knowledge, the city had been sweltering under the hottest of midsummer heats, — 94° in the shade, for example; and now, mittens and overcoats!

I should be sorry to exaggerate, or leave a false impression. In this day of literary conscientiousness, when writers of fiction itself are truth-tellers first, and story-tellers afterwards, — if at all, — it behooves mere tourists and naturalists to speak as under oath. Be it confessed, then, that the foregoing paragraphs, though true in every word, are not to be taken too seriously. If the weather, "the dramatic element in

scenery," happened not to suit the convenience of a naturally selfish man, now ten
times more selfish than usual — as is the
rule — because he was on his annual vacation, it does not follow that it was essentially
bad. The rains were needed, the heat was
to have been expected, and the cold, un-
seasonable and exceptional, was not peculiar
to Tennessee. As for the snow, it was no
more than I have seen before now, even in
Massachusetts, — a week or two earlier in
the month ; and it lent such a glory to the
higher Alleghanies, as we passed them on
our way homeward, that I might cheerfully
have lain shivering for *two* nights in that
unplastered bedroom, with its window that
no man could shut, rather than miss the
spectacle. Eastern Tennessee, I have no
doubt, is a most salubrious country ; prop-
erly recommended by the medical fraternity
as a refuge for consumptive patients. If to
me its meteorological fluctuations seemed
surprisingly wide and sudden, it was perhaps because I had been brought up in the
equable climate of New England. It would
be unfair to judge the world in general by
that favored spot.

The road up the mountain — the " new road," as it is called — is a notable piece of work, done, I was told, by the county chain-gangs. The pleasure of the ascent, which naturally would have been great, was badly diminished by the rain, which made it necessary to keep the sides of the wagon down ; but I was fortunate in my driver. At first he seemed a stolid, uncommunicative body, and when we came to the river I made sure he could not read. As we ·drove upon the bridge, where straight before his eyes was a sign forbidding any one to drive or ride over the bridge at a pace faster than a walk, under a penalty of five dollars for each offense, he whipped up his horse and his mule (the mule the better horse of the two), and they struck into a trot. Halfway across we met another wagon, and its driver too had let his horses out. Illiteracy must be pretty common in these parts, I said to myself. But whatever my driver's educational deficiencies, it did not take long to discover that in his own line he was a master. He could hit the ear of his mule with the end of his whip with a precision that was almost startling. In fact, it *was* startling — to the mule. For my own part, as often as he drew back his hand and let fly the lash, my eye was glued to the mule's right ear in spite of myself. Had my own ears been endowed with life and motion, instead of fastened to my head like blocks of wood, I think they too would have twitched. I wondered how long the man had practiced his art. He appeared to be not more than forty-five years old. Perhaps he came of a race of drivers, and so began life with some hereditary advantages. At all events, he was a specialist, with the specialist's motto, " This one thing I do."

We were hardly off the bridge and in the country before I began plying him with questions about this and that, especially the wayside trees. He answered promptly and succinctly, and turned out to be a man who had kept his eyes open, and, better still, knew how to say, " No, suh," as well as, " Yes, suh." (There is no mark in the dictionaries to indicate the percussive brevity of the vowel sound in " suh " as he pronounced it.) The big tupelo he recognized as the " black-gum." " But is n't it ever called ' sour - gum ' ? " " No, suh." He

knew but one kind of tupelo, as he knew
but one kind of "ellum." There were many
kinds of oaks, some of which he named as
we passed them. This botanical catechism
presently waked up the only other passenger
in the wagon, a modest girl of ten or twelve
years. She too, it appeared, had some acquaintance with trees. I had asked the
driver if there were no long-leaved pines
hereabout. "No, suh," he said. "But I
think I saw some at Chickamauga the other
day," I ventured. (It was the only place I
did see them, as well as I remember.) "Yes,
sir," put in the girl, "there are a good many
there." "Good for you!" I was ready to
say. It was a pretty rare schoolgirl who,
after visiting a battlefield, could tell what
kind of pines grow on it. Persimmons?
Yes, indeed, the girl had eaten them.
There was a tree by the fence. Had I never
eaten them? She seemed to pity me when
I said "No," but I fancied she would have
preferred to see me begin with one a little
short of ripe.

As for the birds of Walden's Ridge, the
driver said, there were partridges, pheasants,
and turkeys. He had seen ravens, also,

but only in winter, he thought, and never in flocks. His brother had once shot one. About smaller birds he could not profess to speak. By and by he stopped the carriage. "There's a bird now," he said, pointing with his whip. "What do you call that?" It was a summer tanager, I told him, or summer redbird. Did he know another redbird, with black wings and tail? Yes, he had seen it; that was the male, and this all-red one was the female. Oh no, I explained; the birds were of different species, and the females in both cases were yellow. He did not insist, — it was a case of a driver and his fare; but he had always been told so, he said, and I do not flatter myself that I convinced him to the contrary. It is hard to believe that one man can be so much wiser than everybody else. A Massachusetts farmer once asked me, I remember, if the night-hawk and the whippoorwill were male and female of the same bird. I answered, of course, that they were not, and gave, as I thought, abundant reason why such a thing could not be possible. But I spoke as a scribe. "Well," remarked the farmer, when I had finished my story, "some folks *say* they be, but I guess they *ain't*."

With such converse, then, we beguiled the climb to the " Brow," — the top of the cliffs which rim the summit of the mountain, and give it from below a fortified look, — and at last, after an hour's further drive through the dripping woods, came to the hotel at which I was to put up — or with which I was to put up — during my stay on the Ridge.

I had hardly taken the road, the next morning, impatient to see what this little world on a mountain top was like, before I came to a lovely brook making its devious course among big boulders with much pleasant gurgling, in the shadow of mountain laurel and white azalea, — a place highly characteristic of Walden's Ridge, as I was afterwards to learn. Just now, naturally, there was no stopping so near home, though a Kentucky warbler, with his cool, liquid song, did his best to beguile me ; and I kept on my way, past a few houses, a tiny box of a post-office, a rude church, and a few more houses, till just beyond the last one the road dropped into the forest again, as if for good.

And there, all at once I seemed to be in New Hampshire. The land fell away sharply, and at one particular point, through a vista, the forest could be seen sloping down on either side to the gap, beyond which, miles away, loomed a hill, and then, far, far in the distance, high mountains dim with haze. It was like a note of sublimity in a poem that till now had been only beautiful.

From the bottom of the valley came a sound of running water, and between me and the invisible stream a chorus of olive-backed thrushes were singing, — the same simple and hearty strains that, in June and July, echo all day long through the woods of the Crawford Notch. The birds were on their way from the far South, and were happy to find themselves in so homelike a place. Then, suddenly, amid the golden voices of the thrushes, I caught the wiry notes of a warbler. They came from the treetops in the valley, and — so I prided myself upon guessing — belonged to a cerulean warbler, a bird of which I had seen my first and only specimen a week before, on Lookout Mountain. Down the steep hillside I scrambled, — New Hampshire clean forgotten, — and was just bringing my glass into play when the fellow took wing, and began singing at the very point I had just left. I hastened back; he flew again, farther up the hill, and again I put myself out of breath with pursuing him. Again and again he sang, now in this tree, now in that, but there was no getting sight of him. The trees should have been shorter, or the bird larger. Straight upward I gazed, till the muscles of my neck cried for mercy. At last I saw him, flitting amid the dense foliage, but so far above me, and so exactly between me and the sun, that I might as well not have seen him at all.

It was a foolish half-hour. The bird, as I afterwards discovered, was nothing but a blue yellow-back, with an original twist to his song. In Massachusetts, I should not have listened to it twice, but on new hunting-grounds a man is bound to look for new game; else what would be the use of traveling? It was a foolish half-hour, I say; but I wish some moralist would explain, in a manner not inconsistent with the dignity of human nature, how it happens that foolish half-hours are commonly so much more

enjoyable at the time, and so much pleasanter in the retrospect, than many that are
more reasonably employed.

I swallowed my disappointment, and
presently forgot it, for at the first turn in
the road I found myself following the
course of a brook or creek, between which
and myself was a dense thicket of mountain
laurel and rhododendron, with trees and
other shrubs intermingled. The laurel was
already in full bloom, while the rhododendrons held aloft clusters of gorgeous rose-
purple buds, a few of which, the middle ones
of the cluster, were just bursting into flower.
Here was beauty of a new order, — such
wealth and splendor of color in surroundings
so romantic. And the place, besides, was
alive with singing birds : hooded warblers,
Kentucky warblers, a Canadian warbler, a
black-throated blue, a black-throated green,
a blue yellow-back, scarlet tanagers, wood
pewees, wood thrushes, a field sparrow (on
the hillside beyond) a cardinal, a chat, a
bunch of white-throated sparrows, and who
could tell what else ? It was an exciting
moment. Luckily, a man can look and
listen both at once. Here was a fringe-

tree, a noble specimen, hung with creamy-white plumes; here was a magnolia, with big leaves and big flowers; and here was a flowering dogwood, not to be put out of countenance in any company; but especially, here were the rhododendrons! And all the while, deep in the thickest of the bushes, some unknown bird was singing a strange, breathless jumble of a song, note tripping over note, — like an eager church-man with his responses, I kept saying to myself, with no thought of disrespect to either party. It cost me a long vigil and much patient coaxing to make the fellow out, and he proved to be merely a Wilson's blackcap, after all; but he was the only bird of his kind that I saw in Tennessee.

On this first visit I did not get far beyond the creek, through the bed of which the road runs, with a single log for foot-passengers. I had spent at least an hour in going a hundred rods, and it was already drawing near dinner time. But I returned to the spot that very afternoon, and half a dozen times afterward. So poor a traveler am I, so ill fitted to explore a new country. Whenever nothing in particular offered

itself, why, it was always pretty down at
Falling Water Creek. There I saw the
rhododendrons come into exuberant bloom,
and there I oftenest see them in memory,
though I found them elsewhere in greater
abundance, and in a setting even more
romantic.

More romantic, perhaps, but hardly more
beautiful. I remember, just beyond the
creek, a bank where sweet bush (*Calycan-
thus*), wild ginger (*Asarum*), rhododendron,
laurel, and plenty of trailing arbutus (the
last now out of flower) were growing side
by side, — a rare combination of beauty
and fragrance. And within a few rods of
the same spot I sat down more than once to
take a long look at a cross-vine covering a
dead hemlock. The branches of the tree,
shortening regularly to the top, were draped
heavily with gray lichens, while the vine,
keeping mostly near the trunk and climbing
clean to the tip, — fifty feet or more, as I
thought, — was hung throughout with large,
orange-red, gold-lined bells. Their numbers
were past guessing. Here and there a
spray of them swung lightly from the end of
a branch, as if inviting the breeze to lend

them motion and a voice. The sight was worth going miles to see, and yet I passed it three times before it caught my eye, so full were the woods of things to look at. After all, *is* it a poor traveler who turns again and again into the same path? Whether is better, to read two good books once, or one good book twice?

A favorite shorter walk, at odd minutes, — before breakfast and between showers, — was through the woods for a quarter of a mile to a small clearing and a cabin. On a Sunday afternoon I ventured to pass the gate and make a call upon my neighbors. The doors of the house stood open, but a glance inside showed that there was no one there, and I walked round it, inspecting the garden, — corn, beans, and potatoes coming on, — till, just as I was ready to turn back into the woods, I descried a man and woman on the hillside not far away; the man leading a mule, and the woman picking strawberries. At sight of a stranger the woman fell behind, but the man kept on to the house, greeted me politely, and invited me to be seated under the hemlock, where two chairs were already placed. After tying

the mule he took the other chair, and we fell
into talk about the weather, the crops, and
things in general. When the wife finally
appeared, I rose, of course; but she went on
in silence and entered the house, while the
husband said, "Oh, keep your seat." We
continued our conversation till the rain began to fall. Then we picked up our chairs
and followed the woman inside. She sat in
the middle of the room (young, pretty, newly
married, and Sunday-dressed), but never
once opened her lips. Her behavior was in
strict accordance with local etiquette, I was
afterward assured (as if *all* etiquette were
not local); but though I admire feminine
modesty as much as any man, I cannot say
that I found this particular manifestation of
it altogether to my liking. Silence is golden,
no doubt, and gold is more precious than
silver, but in cases of this figurative sort I
profess myself a bimetallist. A *little* silver,
I say; enough for small change, at any rate;
and if we can have a pretty free coinage,
why, so much the better, though as to that,
it must be admitted, a good deal depends
upon the "image and superscription." However, my hostess followed her lights, and

reserved her voice — soft and musical let us hope — for her husband's ear.

They had not lived in the house very long, he told me, and he did not know how many years the land had been cleared. There was a fair amount of game in the woods, — turkeys, squirrels, pheasants, and so on, — and in winter the men did considerable hunting. Formerly there were a good many deer, but they had been pretty well killed off. Turkeys still held out. They were gobbling now. His father had been trying for two or three weeks, off and on, to shoot a certain old fellow who had several hens with him down in the valley. His father could call with his mouth better than with any "caller," but so far the bird had been too sharp for him. The son laughed good-naturedly when I confessed to an unsportsmanlike sympathy with the gobbler.

The cabin, built of hewn logs, with clay in the chinks, was neatly furnished, with beds in two corners of the one room, a stone chimney, two doors directly opposite each other, and no window. The doors, it is understood, are always to be open, for ventilation and light. Such is the custom; and custom is nowhere more powerful than in small rustic communities. If a native, led away by his wife, perhaps, puts a window into his new cabin, the neighbors say, "Oh, he is building a glass house, is n't he?" It must be an effeminate woman, they think, who cannot do her cooking and sewing by the light of the door. None the less, in a climate where snow is possible in the middle of May, such a Spartan arrangement must sometimes be found a bit uncomfortable by persons not to the manner born. A preacher confided to me that in his pastoral calls he had once or twice made bold to push to a door directly at his back, when the wind was cold; but the innovation was ill received, and the inmates of the house, doubtless without wishing to hurt their minister's feelings, — since he had meant no harm, to be sure, but was simply unused to the ways of the world, — speedily found some excuse for rectifying his mistake. Probably there is no corner of the world where the question of fresh air and draughts is not available for purposes of moral discipline.

Beside the path to the cabin, on the 13th of May, was a gray-cheeked thrush, a very gray specimen, sitting motionless in the best of lights. " Look at me," he seemed to say. "I am no olive-back. My cheeks are not sallow." On the same day, here and in another place, I saw white-throated sparrows. Their presence at this late hour was a great surprise, and suggested the possibility of their breeding somewhere in the Carolina mountains, though I am not aware that such an occurrence has ever been recorded. Another recollection of this path is of a snow-white milkweed (*Asclepias variegata*), — white with the merest touch of purple to set it off, — for the downright elegance of which I was not in the least prepared. The queen of all milkweeds, surely.

After nightfall the air grew loud with the cries of batrachians and insects, an interesting and novel chorus. On my first evening at the hotel I was loitering up the road, with frequent auditory pauses, thinking how full the world is of unseen creatures which find their day only after the sun goes down, when in a woody spot I heard behind me a sound of footsteps. A woman was close at my heels, fetching a pail of water from the spring. I remarked upon the many voices.

She answered pleasantly. It was the big frogs that I heard, she reckoned.

"Do you have whippoorwills here?" I asked.

"Plenty of 'em," she answered, "plenty of 'em."

"Do you hear them right along the road?"

"Yes, sir; oh yes."

We had gone hardly a rod further before we exclaimed in the same breath, "There is one now!"

I inquired if there was another bird here, something like the whippoorwill, meaning the chuck-will's-widow. But she said no; she knew of but one.

"How early does the whippoorwill get here?" said I.

"Pretty early," she answered.

"By the first of April, should you say?"

"Yes, sir, I think about then. I know the timber is just beginning to put out when they begin to holler."

This mannerly treatment of a stranger was more Christian-like than the stately silence of my lady of the cabin, it seemed to me. I liked it better, at all events. I had learned nothing, perhaps; but unless a man

is far gone in philosophy he need not feel
bound to increase in wisdom every time a
neighbor speaks to him ; and anyhow, that
expression about the " putting out of the
timber " had given me pleasure. Hearing
it thus was better than finding it upon a
page of Stevenson, or some other author
whose business in life is the picking of right
words. Let us have some silver, I repeat.
I am ready to believe, what I have somewhere read, that men will have to give
account not only for every idle word, but
for every idle silence.

The summit of the Ridge, as soon as one
leaves its precipitous rocky edge, — the
Brow, so called, — is simply an indefinite
expanse of gently rolling country, thin-soiled,
but well watered, and covered with fine open
woods, rambling through which the visitor
finds little to remind him of his elevation
above the world. I heard a resident speak
of going to the " top of the mountain," however, and on inquiry learned that a certain
rocky eminence, two miles, more or less,
from Fairmount (the little " settlement "
where I was staying), went by that name,
and was supposed to be the highest point of

the Ridge. My informant kindly made me a rough map of the way thither, and one morning I set out in that direction. It would be shameful to live for a week on the " summit " of a mountain, and not once go to the " top."

The glory of Walden's Ridge, as compared with Lookout Mountain, — so the dwellers there say, — is its streams and springs; and my morning path soon brought me to the usual rocky brook bordered with mountain laurel, holly, and hemlock. To my New England eyes it was an odd circumstance, the hemlocks growing always along the creeks in the valley bottoms. Beyond this point I passed an abandoned cabin, — no other house in sight, — and by and by a second one, near which, in the garden (better worth preserving than the house, it appeared), a woman and two children were at work. Yes, the woman said, I was on the right path. I had only to keep a straight course, and I should bring up at the " top of the mountain." A little farther, and my spirits rose at the sight of a circular, sedgy, woodland pond, such a place as I had not seen in all this Chattanooga country. It ought to yield something new for my local

ornithological list, which up to this time included ninety species, and not one of them
a water-bird. I did my best, beating round
the edge and " squeaking," but startled nothing rarer than a hooded warbler and a
cardinal grosbeak.

Next I traversed a long stretch of unbroken oak woods, with single tall pines interspersed ; and then all at once the path
turned to the right, and ran obliquely down-
hill to a clearing in which stood a house, —
not a cabin, — with a garden, orchard trees,
and beehives. This should be the German
shoemaker's, I thought, looking at my map.
If so, I was pretty near the top, though
otherwise there was no sign of it ; and if I
had made any considerable ascent, it had
been as children increase in stature, — and
as the good increase in goodness, — uncon-
sciously. A woman of some years was in
the garden, and at my approach came up
to the fence, — a round-faced, motherly
body. Yes, the top of the mountain was
just beyond. I could not miss it.

" You do not live here ? " she asked.

No, I explained ; I was a stranger on the
Ridge, — a stranger from Boston.

" From Washington ? "

" No, from Boston."

" Oh ! from Boston ! — Massachusetts ! — Oh-h-h ! "

She would go part way with me, she said, lest I should miss the path. Perhaps she wished to show some special hospitality to a man from Massachusetts ; or possibly she thought I must be more in danger of getting bewildered, being so far from home. But I could not think of troubling her. Was there a spring near by, where I could drink?

" I have water in the house," she answered.

" But is n't there a creek down in the valley ahead ? "

Oh yes, there was a creek ; but had I anything to drink out of ? I thanked her. Yes, I had a cup. " My husband will be at home by the time you come back," she said, as I started on, and I promised to call.

The scene at the brook, halfway between the German's house and the top, would of itself have paid me for my morning's jaunt. I stood on a boulder in mid-current, in the shadow of overhanging trees, and drank it in. Such rhododendrons and laurel, now in the perfection of their beauty! One rhododendron bush was at least ten feet high, and loaded with blooms. Another lifted its crown of a dozen rose-purple clusters amid the dark foliage of a hemlock. A magnolia-tree stood near; but though it was much taller than the laurel or the rhododendron, and had much larger flowers, it made little show beside them. Birds were singing on all hands, and numbers of gay-colored butterflies flitted about, sipping here and there at a blossom. I remember especially a fine tiger swallow-tail; the only one I saw in Tennessee, I believe. I remember, too, how well the rhododendron became him. Here, as in many other places, the laurel was nearly white; a happy circumstance, as it and the rhododendron went the more harmoniously together. Even in this high company, some tufts of cinnamon fern were not to be overlooked; the fertile cinnamon-brown fronds were now at their loveliest, and showed as bravely here, I thought, as in the barest of Massachusetts swamp-lands.

A few rods more, up a moderate slope, and I was at the top of the mountain, — a wall of outcropping rocks, falling off abruptly on the further side, and looking almost like an artificial rampart. Beyond me, to my surprise, I heard the hum of cicadas, — seventeen-year locusts, — a sound of which the lower country had for some time been full, but of which, till this moment, I had heard nothing on the Ridge.

As for the prospect, it was far reaching, but only in one direction, and through openings among the trees. Directly before me, some hundreds of feet below, was a piece of road, with a single cabin and a barn ; and much farther away were other cabins, each with its private clearing. Elsewhere the foreground was an unbroken forest. For some time I could not distinguish the Ridge itself from the outlying world. Mountains and hills crowded the hazy horizon, range beyond range. Moving along the rocks, I found a vista through which Chattanooga and Lookout Mountain were visible. Another change, and a stretch of the Tennessee River came into sight, and, beyond it, Missionary Ridge with its settlements and its two observatories. Evidently I was considerably above the level of the Brow ; but whether this was really the top of the mountain — reached, in some mysterious way, without going uphill — was more than I could say.[1]

Nor did it matter. I was glad to be there. It was a pleasant place and a pleasant hour, with an oak root for a seat, and never an insect to trouble me. That, by the way, was true of all those Tennessee forests, — when I was there, I mean ; from what I heard, the ticks and jiggers must be bad enough later in the season. As men do at such times, — for human nature is of noble origin, and feels no surprise at being well treated, — I took my immunity as a matter of course, and only realized how I had been favored when I got back to Massachusetts, where, on my first visit to the woods, I was fairly driven out by swarms of mosquitoes.

The shoemaker was at home when I reached his house on my return, and at the urgent invitation of himself and his wife I joined them on the piazza for a bit of neighborly chat. I found him a smallish man,

[1] It was *not* the top of the mountain ; so I am now informed, on the best of authority. I followed the map, but misunderstood the man who drew it. It was a map of some other route, and I did not see the top of the mountain, after all.

not German in appearance, but looking, I
thought, like Thoreau, only grown a little
older. He had been on Walden's Ridge for
fifteen years. Before that he was in South
Carolina, but the yellow fever came along
and made him feel like getting out. Yes,
this was a healthy country. He had nothing
to complain of ; he was sixty-two years old
and his doctors' bills had never amounted to
" five dollar."

" Do *you* like living here ? " I asked his
wife.

" No," she answered promptly ; " I never
did. But then," she added, " we can't help
it. If you own something, you know, you
have to stay."

The author of Walden would have appreciated that remark. There was no shoe-
making to be done here, the man said, his
nearest neighbor being half a mile distant
through the woods ; and there was no clover,
so that his bees did not do very well ; and
the frost had just killed all his peach-trees ;
but when I asked if he never felt homesick
for Germany, the answer came like a pistol
shot, — " No."

I inquired about a cave, of which I had

heard reports. Yes, it was a good cave, they said; I could easily find it. But their directions conveyed no very clear idea to my mind, and by and by the woman began talking to her husband in German. "She is telling him he ought to go with me and show me the way," I said to myself; and the next moment she came back to English. "He will go with you," she said. I demurred, but he protested that he could do it as well as not. "Take up a stick; you might see a snake," his wife called after him, as we left the house. He smiled, but did not follow her advice, though I fancied he would have done so had she gone along with us. A half-mile or so through the pathless woods brought us to the cave, which might hold a hundred persons, I thought. The dribbling "creek" fell over it in front. Then the man took me to my path, pointed my way homeward, and, with a handshake (the silver lining of which was not refused, though I had been troubled with a scruple), bade me good-by. First, however, he told me that if I found any one in Boston who wanted to buy a place on Walden's Ridge, he would sell a part of his

or the whole of it. I remember him most
kindly, and would gladly do him a service.
If any reader, having a landed investment
in view, should desire my intervention in
the premises, I am freely at his command ;
only let him bear in mind the terms of the
deed : " If you own something, you know,
you have to stay."

II.

Fairmount, as has already been said, is
but a clearing in the forest. Instead of a
solitary cabin, as elsewhere, there are perhaps a dozen or two of cabins and houses
scattered along the road, which emerges
from the woods at one end of the settlement,
and, after a mile or so in the sun, drops
into them again at the other end. The
glory of the place, and the reason of its
being, as I suppose, is a chalybeate spring
in a woody hollow before the post-office.
There may be a shop of some kind, also,
but memory retains no such impression.
One building, rather larger than most of
its neighbors, and apparently unoccupied, I
looked at more than once with a measure
of that curiosity which is everywhere the

stranger's privilege. It sat squarely on the
road, and boasted a sort of portico or piazza,
— it puzzled me what to call it, — but there
was no vestige of a chimney. One day a
ragged, bright-faced boy met me at the right
moment, and I asked, "Did some one use
to live in that house?" "That?" said he,
in a tone I shall never forget. "That's a
barn. That over there is the dwelling."
My ignorance was fittingly rebuked, and I
had no spirit to inquire about the piazza.
Probably it was nothing but a lean-to.
Even in my humiliation, however, it pleased
me to hear what I should have called that
good literary word "dwelling" on such lips.
A Yankee boy might have said "dwelling-
house," but no Yankee of any age, or none
that I have ever known, would have said
"dwelling," though he might have read the
word in books a thousand times. I thought
of a spruce colored waiter in Florida, who,
when I asked him at breakfast how the day
was likely to turn out, answered promptly,
"I think it will be inclement." It may
reasonably be counted among the minor
advantages of travel that it enriches one's
every-day vocabulary.

Another Fairmount building (an unmistakable house, this time) is memorable to me because on the doorstep, day after day, an old gentleman and a younger antagonist — they might have been grandfather and grandson — were playing checkers. " I hope you are beating the young fellow," I could not help saying once to the old gentleman. He smiled dubiously, and made some halting reply suggestive of resignation rather than triumph ; and it came to me with a kind of pang, as I passed on, that if growing old is a bad business, as most of us think, it is perhaps an unfavorable symptom when a man finds himself, not out of politeness, but as a simple matter of course, taking sides with the aged.

Fairmounters, living in the woods, have no outlook upon the world. If they wish to see off, they must go to the Brow, which, by a stroller's guess, may be two miles distant. My first visit to it was the pleasanter — the more vacational, so to speak — for being an accident. I sauntered aimlessly down the road, past the scattered houses and orchards (the raising of early apples seemed to be a leading industry on the Ridge, though a

Chattanooga gentleman had assured me that
the principal crops were blackberries and
rabbits), and almost before I knew it, was
in the same delightful woods that had welcomed me wherever I had gone. And in
the same woods the same birds were singing.
My notes make particular record of hooded
and Kentucky warblers, these being two of
my newer acquaintances, as well as two of
the commoner Ridge songsters ; but I halted
for some time, and with even a livelier interest, to listen to an old friend (no acquaintance, if you please), — a black-throated
green warbler. It was one of the queerest
of songs : a bar of five or six notes, uniform
in pitch, and then at once, in perfect form
and voice, — the voice being a main part of
the music in the case of this warbler, —
the familiar *trees, trees, murmuring trees.*
Where could the fellow have picked up such
a ditty? No doubt there was some story
connected with it. Nothing is born of itself.
A dozen years ago, in the Green Mountains,
— at Bread-Loaf Inn, — I heard from the
forest by the roadside a song utterly strange,
and hastened in search of its author. After
much furtive approach and diligent scanning

of the foliage, I had the bird under my
opera-glass, — a black-throated blue warbler! With my eye still upon him, he sang
again and again, and the song bore no faint-
est resemblance to the *kree, kree, kree,* which
all New England bird-lovers know as the
work of *Dendroica cærulescens.* In what
private school he had been educated I have.
no idea; but I believe that every such
extreme eccentricity goes back to something out of the common in the bird's early
training.

I felt in no haste. Life is easy in the
Tennessee mountains. A pile of lumber,
newly unloaded near the road, — in the
woods, of course, — offered a timely seat,
and I took it. Some Chattanooga gentleman was planning a summer cottage for
himself, I gathered. May he enjoy it for
twenty years as much as I did for twenty
minutes. Not far beyond, near a fork in the
road, a man of twenty-five or thirty, a youth
of sixteen or seventeen, and a small boy were
playing marbles in a cabin yard. I interrupted the sport long enough to inquire
which road I had better take. I was going
nowhere in particular, I explained, and

wanted simply a pleasant stroll. "Then I would go to the Brow, if I were you," said the man. "Keep a straight road. It is n't far." I thanked him, and with a cheery "Come on!" to his playmates he ran back, literally, to the ring. Yes, life is easy in the Tennessee mountains. It is not to be assumed, nevertheless, that the man was a do-nothing: probably he had struck work for a few minutes only; but, like a sensible player, he was enjoying the game while it lasted. Perhaps it is a certain inborn Puritanical industriousness, against which I have never found the courage effectually to rebel, that makes me look back upon this dooryard comedy as one of the brightest incidents of my Tennessee vacation. Fancy a Massachusetts farmer playing marbles at nine o'clock in the forenoon!

At that moment, it must be owned, a rebuke of idleness would have fallen with a poor grace from my Massachusetts lips. If the player of marbles had followed his questioner round the first turn, he would have seen him standing motionless beside a swamp, holding his head on one side as if listening, — though there was nothing to be heard, —

or evoking ridiculous squeaking noises by sucking idiotically the back of his hand. Well, I was trying to find another bird, just as he was trying to knock another marble out of the ring.

The spot invited such researches, — a bushy swamp, quite unlike the dry woods and rocky woodland brooks which I had found everywhere else. I had seen my first cerulean warbler on Lookout Mountain, my first Cape May warbler on Cameron Hill, my first Kentucky warbler on Missionary Ridge, and my first blue-winged yellow warbler at the Chickamauga battlefield. If Walden was to treat me equally well, as in all fairness it ought, now was the time. Looking, listening, and squeaking were alike unrewarded, however, till I approached the same spot on my return. Then some bird sang a new song. I hoped it was a prothonotary warbler, a bird I had never seen, and about whose notes I knew nothing. More likely it was a Louisiana water-thrush, a bird I had seen, but had never heard sing. Whichever it was, alas, it speedily fell silent, and no beating of the bush proved of the least avail.

Meanwhile I had been to the Brow, where I had sat for an hour or more on the edge of the mountain, gazing down upon the world. The sky was clouded, but here and there were fugitive patches of sunshine, now on Missionary Ridge, now on the river, now glorifying the smoke of the city. Southward, just across the valley and over Chattanooga, was Lookout Mountain; eastward stretched Missionary Ridge, with many higher hills behind it; and more to the north, and far in the distance, loomed the Great Smoky Mountains, in all respects true to their name. The valley at my feet was beautiful beyond words: green forests interspersed with green clearings, lonely cabins, and bare fields of red earth. At the north, Walden's Ridge made a turn eastward, narrowing the valley, but without ending it. Chimney swifts were cackling merrily, and the air was full of the hum of seventeen-year locusts, — miles and miles of continuous sound. From somewhere far below rose the tinkle of cowbells. Even on that cloudy and smoky day it was a glorious landscape; but it pleased me afterward to remember that the eye returned of itself again and again to a stretch of freshly green meadow along a slender watercourse, — a valley within the valley. Of all the fair picture, that was the most like home.

Meanwhile there was no forgetting that undiscovered stranger in the swamp. Whoever he was, he must be made to show himself; and the next day, when the usual noonday deluge was past, I looked at the clouds, and said : "We shall have another, but in the interval I can probably reach the Brow. There I will take shelter on the piazza of an unoccupied cottage, and, when the rain is over, go back to the swamp, see my bird, and thence return home." So it turned out — in part. The clouds hurried me, but I reached the Brow just in season, climbed the cottage fence, the gate being padlocked, and, thoroughly heated as I was, paced briskly to and fro on the piazza in a chilling breeze for an hour or more, the flood all the while threatening to fall, and the thunder shaking the house. There was plenty to look at, for the cottage faced the Great Smokies, and though we were under the blackest of clouds, the landscape below was largely in the sun. The noise of the

locusts was incessant. Nothing but the peals
of thunder kept it out of my ears.

So far, then, my plans had prospered;
but to find the mysterious bird, — that was
not so easy. The swamp was silent, and I
was at once so cold and so hot, and so badly
under the weather already, that I dared not
linger.

In the woods, nevertheless, I stopped long
enough to enjoy the music of a master
cardinal, — a bewitching song, and, as I
thought, original : *birdy*, *birdy*, repeated
about ten times in the sweetest of whistles,
and then a sudden descent in the pitch, and
the same syllables over again. At that
instant, a Carolina wren, as if stirred to
rivalry, sprang into a bush and began
whistling *cherry*, *cherry*, *cherry* at his
loudest and prettiest. It was a royal duet.
The cardinal was in magnificent plumage,
and a scarlet tanager near by was equally
handsome. If the tanager could whistle
like the cardinal, our New England woods
would have a bird to brag of.

Not far beyond these wayside musicians I
came upon a boy sitting beside a wood-pile,
with his saw lying on the ground. " It is

easier to sit down than to saw wood, is n't it?" said I. Possibly he was unused to such aphoristic modes of speech. He took time to consider. Then he smiled, and said, "Yes, sir." The answer was all-sufficient. We spoke from experience, both of us; and between men who *know*, whatever the matter in hand, disagreement is impossible and amplification needless.

Three days later — my last day on the Ridge — I had better luck at the swamp. The stranger was singing on the nearer edge as I approached, and I had simply to draw near and look at him, — a Louisiana water-thrush. He sang, and I listened; and farther along, at the little bridge where I had first heard the song, another like him was in tune. The strain, as warbler songs go ("water-thrushes" being not thrushes, but warblers), is rather striking, — clear, pretty loud, of about ten notes, the first pair of which are longest and best. I speak of what I heard, and give, of course, my own impression. Audubon pronounces the notes "as powerful and mellow, and at times as varied," as those of the nightingale, and Wilson waxes almost equally enthusiastic in his praise of the "exquisitely sweet and expressive voice." Here, as in Florida, I was interested to perceive how instantly the bird's appearance and carriage distinguished it from its Northern relative, although the descriptions of the two species, as given in books, sound confusingly alike. It is matter for thankfulness, perhaps, that language is not yet so all-expressive as to render individual eyesight superfluous.

I kept on to the Brow, and some time afterward was at Mabbitt's Spring, quenching my thirst with a draught of liquid iron rust, when a third songster of the same kind struck up his tune. The spring, spurting out of the rock in a slender jet, is beside the same stream — Little Falling Water — that makes through the swamp; and along its banks, it appeared, the water-thrushes were at home. I was glad to have heard the famous singer, but my satisfaction was not without alloy. Walden, after all, had failed to show me a new bird, though it had given me a new song.

The most fatiguing, and perhaps the most interesting of my days on the Ridge was the one day in which I did not travel on

foot. Passing through the village, on my
return from one of my earlier visits to
Falling Water, I stopped a nice-looking
man (if he will pardon the expression,
copied from my notes), driving a horse with
a pair of clothes-line reins. He had an air
of being at home, and naturally I took him
for a native. Would he tell me something
about the country, especially about the
roads, so that I might improve my scanty
time to the best advantage? Very glably,
he answered. He had walked and driven
over the mountain a good deal, surveying,
and if I would call at his house, a short distance down the road, — the house with the
big barn, — he would make me a rough map,
such as would answer my purpose. At the
same time he mentioned two or three shorter
excursions which I ought not to miss ; and
when I had thanked him for his kindness,
he gathered up the reins and drove on.
Intending no disrespect to the inhabitants of
the Ridge, I may perhaps be allowed to say
that I was considerably impressed by a certain unexpected propriety, and even elegance, of diction, on the part of my new
acquaintance. I remember in particular his

description of a pleasant cold spring as being situated not far from the "confluence" of two streams. *Con-fluens*, I thought, flowing together. Having always something else to do, I omitted to call at his house, and one day, when we met again in the road, I apologized for my neglect, and asked another favor. He was familiar with the country, and kept a horse. Could he not spare a day to take me about? If he thought this proposal a bit presumptuous, courtesy restrained him from letting the fact be seen, and, after a few minutes of deliberation, — his hands being pretty full just then, he explained, — he promised to call for me two mornings later, at seven o'clock. We would take a luncheon along, and make a day of it.

He appeared at the gate in due season, and in a few minutes we were driving over a road new to me, but through the same spacious oak woods to which I had grown accustomed. We went first to Burnt Cabin Spring, one of the famous chalybeate springs of the mountain, — a place formerly frequented by picnic parties, but now, to all appearance, fallen into neglect. We stretched

our legs, drank of the water, admired the
flowers and ferns, talking all the while (it
was here that my companion told a story of
a young theologian from Grant University,
who, in a solemn discourse, spoke repeatedly
of Jacob as having "euchred his brother
out of his birthright"), and then, while a
"pheasant" drummed near by, took our
places again in the buggy.

Another stage, still through the oak
woods, and we were at Signal Point, famous
— in local tradition, at least — as the station
from which General Sherman signaled encouragement to the Union army beleaguered
in Chattanooga, in danger of starvation or
surrender. I had looked at the bold, jut-
ting crags from Lookout Mountain and elsewhere, and rejoiced at last to stand upon them.

It would have been delightful to spend
a long day there, lying upon the cliffs and
enjoying the prospect, which, without being
so far-reaching as from Point Lookout, or
even from the eastern brim of Walden, is
yet extensive and surpassingly beautiful.
The visitor is squarely above the river,
which here, in the straitened valley between
the Ridge and Raccoon Mountain, grows

narrower and narrower till it rushes through
the " Suck." Even at that elevation we
could hear the roar of the rapids. A short
distance above the Suck, and almost at
our feet, lay Williams Island. A farmer's
Eden it looked, with its broad, newly
planted fields, and its house surrounded by
outbuildings and orchard-trees. The view
included Chattanooga, Missionary Ridge,
and much else; but its special charm was
its foreground, the part peculiar to itself, —
the valley, the river, and Raccoon Mountain.
Along the river-banks were small clearings,
each with its one cabin, and generally a
figure or two ploughing or planting. A
man in a strangely long boat — a dugout,
probably — was making his difficult way
upstream with a paddle. The Tennessee,
in the neighborhood of Chattanooga, at all
events, is too swift for pleasure-boating.
Seen from above, as I commonly saw it, it
looked tranquil enough; but when I came
down to its edge, now and then, the speed
and energetic sweep of the smooth current
laid fast hold upon me. From the mountains
to the sea is a long, long journey, and no
wonder the river felt in haste.

I had gone to Signal Point not as an ornithologist, but as a patriot and a lover of beauty ; but, being there, I added one to my list of Tennessee birds, — a red-tailed hawk, one of the very few hawks seen in all my trip. Sailing below us, it displayed its rusty, diagnostic tail, and put its identity at once beyond question.

Our next start — far too speedy, for the day was short — was for Williams Point ; but on our way thither we descended into the valley of Shoal Creek, down which, with the creek to keep it company, runs the old mountain road, now disused and practically impassable. Here we hitched the horse, and strolled downwards for perhaps half a mile. I was never in a lovelier spot. The mountain brook, laughing over the stones, is overhung with laurel and rhododendron, which in turn are overhung by precipitous rocks broken into all wild and romantic shapes, with here and there a cavern — " rock-house " — to shelter a score of travelers. The place was rich in ferns and other plants, which, unhappily, I had no time to examine, and all the particulars of which have faded out of my memory. We walked far enough to look over the edge of the mountain, and up to the Signal Point cliffs. If I could have stayed there two or three hours, it would have been a memorable season. As it was, the stroll was enlivened by one little adventure, at which I have laughed too many times ever to forget it.

I had been growing rapturous over the beauty of things, when my companion said, " There are some people whom it is no pleasure to take into places like this. They can't keep their eyes off the ground, they are so bitten with the fear of snakes." He was a few paces ahead of me, as he spoke, and the sentence was barely finished before he shouted, " Look at that huge snake!" and sprang forward to snatch up a stone. " Get a stick!" he cried. " Get a stick!" From his manner I took it for granted that the creature was a rattlesnake, and a glance at it, lying motionless among the stones beside the road, did not undeceive me. I turned hurriedly, looking for a stick, but somehow could not find one, and in a moment more was recalled by shouts of " Come and help me! It will get away from us!" It was a question of life and death, I thought, and I ran forward and began throwing stones. " Look out! Look out! You 'll bury it!" cried my companion; but just then one of my shots struck the snake squarely in the head. "That 's a good one!" exclaimed the other man, and, picking up a dead stick, he thrust it under the disabled creature and tossed it into the road. Then he bent over it, and, with a stone, pounded its head to a jelly. Such a fury as possessed him! He might have been bruising the head of Satan himself, as no doubt he was — in his mind; for my surveyor was also a preacher, as had already transpired.

" It is n't a venomous snake, is it?" I ventured to ask, when the work was done.

" Oh, I think not," and he pried open its jaws to look for its fangs.

" I don't generally kill innocent snakes," I ventured again, a little inopportunely, it must be confessed.

" Well, *I* do," said the preacher. " The very sight of a snake stirs my hatred to its depths."

After that it was natural to inquire whether he often saw rattlesnakes hereabouts. (The driver who brought me up the mountain had said that they were not common, but that I "wanted to look out sharp for them in the woods.") My companion had never seen one, he answered, but his wife had once killed one in their dooryard. Then, by way of cooling off, after the fervor of the conflict, he told me about a gentleman and his little boy, who, having come to spend a vacation on the Ridge, started out in the morning for a stroll. They were quickly back again, and the boy, quite out of breath, came running into the garden.

"Oh, Mr. M.," he cried, "we saw a rattlesnake, and papa fired off his pistol!"

"A rattlesnake! Where is it? What did it look like?"

"Why, we did n't see it, but we heard it."

"What was the noise like?" asked Mr. M., and he took a pencil from his pocket and began tapping on a log.

"That's it!" said the boy, "that's it!"

They had heard a woodpecker drilling for grubs, — or drumming for love, — whereupon the man had fired his pistol, and for them there was no more walking in the woods.

After our ramble along Shoal Creek we rested at the ford, near a brilliant show of laurel and rhododendron, and ate our luncheon to the music of the stream. I finished first, as my evil habit is, and was crossing the brook on natural stepping-stones when a bird — a warbler of some unknown kind — saluted me from the thicket. Making my companion a signal not to disturb us by driving into the stream, I gave myself up to discovering the singer; edging this way and that, while the fellow moved about also, always unseen, and sang again and again, now a louder song, now, with charming effect, a quieter and briefer one, till I was almost as badly beside myself as the preacher had been half an hour before. But my warfare was less successful than his, for, with all my pains, I saw not so much as a feather. There is nothing prettier than a jungle of laurel and rhododendron in full bloom, but there are many easier places in which to make out a bird.

Williams Point, which we reached on foot, after driving as near it as the roughness of the unfrequented road would comfortably allow, is not in itself equal to Signal Point, but affords substantially the same magnificent prospect. Near it, in the woods, stood a newly built cabin, looking badly out of place with its glaring unweathered boards; and beside the cabin stood a man and woman in a condition of extreme disgust. The man had come up the mountain to work in some coal-mine, if I understood him correctly; but the tools were not ready, there was no water, his household goods were stranded down in the valley somewhere (the hens were starving to death, the woman added), and, all in all, the pair were in a sorry plight.

Here, as at Signal Point, I made an addition to my local ornithology, and this time too the bird was a hawk. We were standing on the edge of the cliff, when a sparrow hawk, after alighting near us, took wing and hung for some time suspended over the abyss, beating against the breeze, and so holding itself steady, — a graceful piece of work, the better appreciated for being seen from above. Here, also, for the first time in my life, I was addressed as a "you-un." "Where be you-uns from?" asked the woman at the cabin, after the ordinary greetings had been exchanged. I believe, in my innocence, I had always looked upon that word as an invention of story-writers.

Somewhere in this neighborhood we traversed a pine wood, in which my first Walden pine warbler was trilling. Then, for some miles, we drove along the Brow, with the glory of the world — valley, river, and mountain — outspread before us, and the Great Smokies looming in the background, barely visible through the haze. For seven miles, I was told, one could drive along that mountain rim. Surely the city of Chattanooga is happy in its suburbs. Here were many cottages, the greater number as yet unopened; and not far beyond the one under the piazza of which I had weathered the thunderstorm of the day before, the road entered the forest again. Then, as the way grew more and more difficult, we left the horse behind us, and by and by came to a footpath. This brought us at last to Falling Water Fall, where Little Falling Water — after threading the swamp and passing Mabbitt's Spring, as before described — tumbles over a precipice which my companion, with his surveyor's eye, esti-

mated to be one hundred and fifty feet in
height. The slender stream, broken into
jewels as it falls, strikes the bottom at some
distance from the foot of the cliffs, which
here form the arc of a circle, and are not
perpendicular, but deeply hollowed. After
enjoying the prospect from this point, —
holding to a tree and leaning over the edge
of the rocks, — we retraced our steps till we
came to a steep, zigzag path, which took us
to the foot of the precipice. Here, as well
as above, were laurel and rhododendron in
profusion. One big rhododendron-tree grew
on the face of the cliff, thirty feet over our
heads, leaning outward, and bearing at least
fifty clusters of gorgeous rose-purple flowers ;
and a smaller one, in a similiar position,
was equally full. The hanging gardens of
Babylon may have been more wonderful,
but I was well content.

From the point where we stood the ledge
makes eastward for a long distance, almost
at right angles, and the cliffs for a mile —
or, more likely, for two or three miles —
were straight before us, broken everywhere
into angles, light gray and reddish-brown
intermixed, with the late afternoon sun shin-

ing full upon them, and the green forest fringing them above and sweeping away from them below.

It was a breathless clamber up the rocks again, tired and poorly off as I was, but I reached the top with one hand full of rhododendrons (it seemed a shame to pick them, and a shame to leave them), and in half an hour we were driving homeward, our day's work done; while my seatmate, who, besides being preacher, lawyer, surveyor, and farmer, was also a mystic and a saint, — though he would have refused the word, — fell into a strain of reminiscence, appropriate to the hour, about the inner life of the soul, its hopes, its struggles, and its joys. I listened in reverent silence. The passion for perfection is not yet so common as to have become commonplace, and one need not be certain of a theory in order to admire a practice. He had already told me who his father was, and I had ceased to wonder at his using now and then a choice phrase.

My friend (he will allow me that word, I am sure) had given me a day of days, and with it a new idea of this mountain world; where the visitor finds hills and valleys,

creeks and waterfalls, the most beautiful of
forests, with clearings, isolated cabins, strag-
gling settlements, orchards, and gardens,
and where he forgets again and again that
he is on a mountain at all. Even now I had
seen but a corner of it, as I have seen but a
corner of the larger world on which, for
these few years back, I have had what I call
my existence. And even of what I saw,
much has gone undescribed : stately tulip-
trees deep in the forest, with humming-birds
darting from flower to flower among them ;
the flame-colored azalea ; the ground flowers
of the woods, including some tiny yellow
lady's - slippers, too dainty for the foot of
Cinderella herself ; the road to Sawyer's
Springs ; and numbers of birds, whose names,
even, I have omitted. It was a wonderful
world ; but if the hobbyist may take the pen
for a single sentence, it may stand confessed
that the greatest wonder of all was this, —
that in all those miles of oak forest I found
not one blue jay.

Another surprising circumstance, which I
do not remember to have noticed, however,
till my attention was somewhat rudely called
to it, was the absence of colored people.

With the exception of three servants at the hotel, I saw none but whites. Walden's Ridge, although stanchly Union in war-time, and largely Republican now, as I was told, is a white man's country. I had gone to bed one night, and was fast asleep, when I was wakened suddenly by the noise of some one hurrying up the stairs and shouting, "Where's the gun? Where's the gun? Shorty 's been shot!" "Shorty" was the colored waiter, and the speaker was a general factotum, an English boy. The colored people — Shorty, his wife, and the cook — had been out on the edge of the woods behind the house, when three men had fired at them, or pretended to do so. It was explained the next morning that this was only an attempt (on the part of some irresponsible young men, as the older residents said) to "run the niggers off the mountain," — after what I understood to be a somewhat regular custom. "Niggers" did not belong there; their place was down below. If a Chattanooga cottager brought up a colored servant, he was " respectfully requested " to send him back, and save the natives the trouble of attending to the matter. In short, the

Ridgites appeared to look upon "niggers" as Northern laborers look upon non-union men — "scabs."

The hotel-keeper, an Englishman, with an Englishman's notions about personal rights, was naturally indignant. He would hire his own servants, or he would shut the house. In any event, the presence of "Whitecaps," real or imaginary, must affect his summer patronage. I fully expected to see the colored trio pack up and go back to Chattanooga, without waiting for further hints; but they showed no disposition to do anything of the sort, and, I must add, rose in my estimation accordingly.

Of the feeling of the community I had a slight but ludicrous intimation a day or two after the shooting. I passed a boy whom I had noticed in the road, some days before, playing with a pig, lifting him by the hind legs and pitching him over forwards. "He can turn a somerset good," he had said to me, as I passed. Now, for the sake of being neighborly, I asked, "How's the pig to-day?" He smiled, and made some reply, as if he appreciated the pleasantry; but a more serious-looking playmate took up his parable, and said, "The pig 'll be all right, if the folks up at the hotel don't shoot him." His tone and look were intended to be deeply significant. "Oh, I know you," they implied: "you are up at the hotel, where they threaten to shoot white folks."

For my last afternoon — wars and rumors of wars long since forgotten — I went to the place that had pleased me first, the valley of Falling Water Creek. The cross-vine on the dead hemlock had by this time dropped the greater part of its bells, but even yet many were hanging from the uppermost branches. The rhododendron was still at the height of its splendor. All the gardens were nothing to it, I said to myself. Crossing the creek on the log, and the branch on stepping-stones, I went to quench my thirst at the Marshall Spring, which once had a cabin beside it, and frequent visitors, but now was clogged with fallen leaves and seemingly abandoned. It was perhaps more beautiful so. Directly behind it rose a steep bank, and in front stood an oak and a maple, the latter leaning toward it and forming a pointed arch, — a worthy entrance. Mossy stones walled it in, and ferns grew luxuriantly about it. Just over them, an azalea still held two fresh pink flowers, the last till another May. In such a spot it would have been easy to grow sentimental; but there came a rumbling of thunder, the sky darkened, and, with a final hasty look about me, I picked up my umbrella and started homeward.

My last walk had ended like many others in that showery, fragmentary week. But what is bad weather when the time is past? All those black clouds have left no shadow on Walden's Ridge, and the best of all my strolls beside Falling Water, a stroll not yet finished,

"The calm sense of seen beauty without sight,"

suffers no harm. As Thoreau says, "It is after we get home that we really go over the mountain."

SOME TENNESSEE BIRD NOTES.

WHOEVER loves the music of English sparrows should live in Chattanooga; there is no place on the planet, it is to be hoped, where they are more numerous and pervasive. Mocking - birds are scarce. To the best of my recollection, I saw none in the city itself, and less than half a dozen in the surrounding country. A young gentleman whom I questioned upon the subject told me that they used to be common, and attributed their present increasing rarity to the persecution of boys, who find a profit in selling the young into captivity. Their place, in the city especially, is taken by catbirds; interesting, imitative, and in their own measure tuneful, but poor substitutes for mocking-birds. In fact, that is a rôle which it is impossible to think of any bird as really filling. The brown thrush, it is true, sings quite in the mocking-bird's manner, and, to my ear, almost or quite as well; but he possesses no gift as a mimic, and further-

more, without being exactly a bird of the
forest or the wilderness, is instinctively and
irreclaimably a recluse. It would be hard,
even among human beings, to find a nature
less touched with urbanity. In the mocking-bird the elements are more happily
mingled. Not gregarious, intolerant of
rivalry, and, as far as creatures of his own
kind are concerned, a stickler for elbow-
room, — sharing with his brown relative in
that respect, — he is at the same time a
born citizen and neighbor ; as fond of gardens and dooryard trees as the thrasher is
of scrublands and barberry bushes. " Man
delights me," he might say, " and woman
also." He likes to be listened to, it is
pretty certain ; and possibly he is dimly
aware of the artistic value of appreciation,
without which no artist ever did his best.
Add to this endearing social quality the
splendor and freedom of the mocker's vocal
performances, multifarious, sensational, in-
comparable, by turns entrancing and amusing, and it is easy to understand how he has
come to hold a place by himself in Southern
sentiment and literature. A city without
mocking-birds is only half Southern, though

black faces be never so thick upon the side-
walks and mules never so common in the
streets. If the boys have driven the great
mimic away from Chattanooga, it is time
the fathers took the boys in hand. Civic
pride alone ought to bring this about, to
say nothing of the possible effect upon real
estate values of the abundant and familiar
presence of this world-renowned, town-lov-
ing, town-charming songster.

From my window, on the side of Cameron
Hill, I heard daily the singing of an orchard
oriole — another fine and neighborly bird —
and a golden warbler, with sometimes the
fidgety, fidgety of a Maryland yellow-throat.
What could *he* be fussing about in so
unlikely a quarter? An adjoining yard
presented the unnatural spectacle — unnatural, but, I am sorry to say, not unprece-
dented — of a bird-house occupied in part-
nership by purple martins and English
sparrows. They had finished their quarrels,
if they had ever had any, — which can
hardly be open to doubt, both native and
foreigner being constitutionally belligerent,
— and frequently sat side by side upon the
ridge-pole, like the best of friends. The

oftener I saw them there, the more indignant I became at the martins' un-American behavior. Such a disgraceful surrender of the Monroe Doctrine was too much even for a man of peace. I have never called myself a Jingo, but for once it would have done me good to see the lion's tail twisted.

With the exception of a few pairs of rough-wings on Missionary Ridge, the martins seemed to be the only swallows in the country at that time of the year; and though *Progne subis*, in spite of an occasional excess of good nature, is a most noble bird, it was impossible not to feel that by itself it constituted but a meagre representation of an entire family. Swallows are none too numerous in Massachusetts, in these days, and are pretty certainly growing fewer and fewer, what with the prevalence of the box - monopolizing European sparrow, and the passing of the big, old-fashioned, widely ventilated barn; for there is no member of the family, not even the sand martin, whose distribution does not depend in great degree upon human agency. Even yet, however, if a Massachusetts man will make a circuit of a few miles, he will usually

meet with tree swallows, barn swallows, cliff
swallows, sand martins, and purple martins.
In other words, he need not go far to find
all the species of eastern North America,
with the single exception of the least attractive of the six; that is to say, the rough-
wing. As compared with the people of
eastern Tennessee, then, we are still pretty
well favored. It is worth while to travel
now and then, if only to find ourselves better
off at home.

It might be easy to suggest plausible
reasons for the general absence of swallows
from a country like that about Chattanooga;
but the extraordinary scarcity of hawks,
while many persons — not ornithologists —
would account it less of a calamity, is more
of a puzzle. From Walden's Ridge I saw
a single sparrow hawk and a single red-tail;
in addition to which I remember three birds
whose identity I could not determine. Five
hawks in the course of three weeks spent
entirely out of doors, in the neighborhood of
mountains covered with old forest! Taken
by itself, this unexpected showing might
have been ascribed to some queer combination of accidents, or to a failure of observa-

tion. In fact, I was inclined so to explain it till I noticed that Mr. Brewster had chronicled a similar state of things in what is substantially the same piece of country. Writing of western North Carolina, he says : [1] " The general scarcity — one may almost say absence — of hawks in this region during the breeding season is simply unaccountable. Small birds and mammals, lizards, snakes, and other animals upon which the various species subsist are everywhere numerous, the country is wild and heavily forested, and, in short, all the necessary conditions of environment seem to be fulfilled." Certainly, so far as my ingenuity goes, the mystery is " unaccountable ; " but of course, like every other mystery, it would open quickly enough if we could find the key.

Turkey vultures were moderately numerous, — much less abundant than in Florida, — and twice I saw a single black vulture, recognizable, almost as far as it could be seen (but I do not mean at a first glance, nor without due precaution against foreshortened effects), by its docked tail.

The Auk, vol. iii. p. 103.

Both are invaluable in their place,—useful, graceful, admirable, and disgusting. The vultures, the martins, and the swifts were the only common aerial birds. The swifts, happily, were everywhere,— jovial souls in a sooty dress,— and had already begun nest-building. I saw them continually pulling up against the twigs of a partially dead tree near my window. In them nature has developed the bird idea to its extreme,— a pair of wings, with just body enough for ballast; like a racing-yacht, built for nothing but to carry sail and avoid resistance. Their flight is a good visual music, as Emerson might have said; but I love also their quick, eager notes, like the sounds of children at play. And while it has nothing to do with Tennessee, I am prompted to mention here a bird of this species that I once saw in northern New Hampshire on the 1st of October,— an extraordinarily late date, if my experience counts for anything. With a friend I had made an ascent of Mount Lafayette (one of the days of a man's life), and as we came near the Profile House, on our return to the valley, there passed overhead a single chimney swift.

What he could be doing there at that season was more than either of us could divine. It was impossible to feel any great concern about him, however. The afternoon was nearly done, but at the rate he was traveling it seemed as if he might be in Mexico before sunrise. And easily enough he may have been, if Mr. Gätke is right in his contention that birds of very moderate powers of wing are capable of flying all night at the rate of four miles a minute!

The comparative scarcity of crows about Chattanooga, and the amazing dearth of jays in the oak forest of Walden's Ridge, have been touched upon elsewhere. As for the jays, their absence must have been more apparent than real, I am bound to believe. It was their silent time, probably. Still another thing that I found surprising was the small number of woodpeckers. For the first four days I saw not a single representative of the family. It would be next to impossible to be so much out of doors in Massachusetts at any season of the year with a like result. During my three weeks in Tennessee I saw eight flickers, seven hairy woodpeckers, two red-heads, and two

or three red-cockaded woodpeckers, besides
which I heard one downy and one "logcock." The last-named bird, which is big
enough for even the careless to notice,
seemed to be well known to the inhabitants
of Walden's Ridge, where I heard it. By
what they told me, it should be fairly common, but I saw nothing of its "peck-holes."
The first of my two red-headed woodpeckers
was near the base of Missionary Ridge,
wasting his time in exploring pole after pole
along the railway. Did he mistake them
for so many dead trees still standing on
their own roots? Dry and seemingly unde-
cayed, they appeared to me to offer small
encouragement to a grub-seeker ; but probably the fellow knew his own business best.
On questions of economic entomology, I
fear I should prove but a lame adviser for
the most benighted woodpecker that ever
drummed. And yet, being a man, I could
not help feeling that this particular red-
head was behaving uncommonly like a fool.
Was there ever a man who did not take it
as a matter of course that he should be wiser
than the "lower animals" ?

Humming-birds cut but a small figure in

my daily notes till I went to Walden's
Ridge. There, in the forest, they were
noticeably abundant, — for humming-birds,
that is to say. It seemed to be the time of
pairing with them ; more than once the two
sexes were seen together, — an unusual
occurrence, unless my observation has been
unfortunate, after the nest is built, or even
while it is building. One female piqued my
curiosity by returning again and again to
the bole of an oak, hovering before it as
before a flower, and more than once clinging
to its rough upright surface. At first I
took it for granted that she was picking
off bits of lichen with which to embellish
the outer wall of her nest ; but after each
browsing she alighted here or there on a
leafless twig. If she had been gathering
nest material, she would have flown away
with it, I thought.

At another time, in a tangle of shrubbery,
I witnessed a most lively encounter between
two humming-birds ; a case of fighting or
love-making, — two things confusingly alike
to an outsider, — in the midst of which one
of the contestants suddenly· displayed so
dazzling a gorget that for an instant I

mistook it for a scarlet flower. I did not
" wipe my eye," not being a poet, nor even
a " rash gazer," but I admired anew the
wonderful flashing jewel, now coal-black,
now flaming red, with which, perhaps, the
male ruby-throat blinds his long-suffering
mate to all his shameful treatment of her
in her season of watchfulness and motherly
anxiety. Does she never remind him, I
wonder, that there are some things whose
price is far above rubies? I had never
seen the humming-bird so much a forest-
dweller as here, and gladly confessed that
I had never seen him when he looked so
romantically at home and in place. The
tulip-trees, in particular, might have been
made on purpose for him.

As the Chattanooga neighborhood was
poorly supplied with hawks, woodpeckers,
and swallows, so was it likewise with sparrows, though in a less marked degree. The
common species — the only resident species
that I met with, but my explorations were
nothing like complete — were chippers, field
sparrows, and Bachman sparrows ; the first
interesting for their familiarity, the other
two for their musical gifts. In a compari-

son between eastern Tennessee — as I saw it — and eastern Massachusetts, the Bachman sparrow must be set against the song sparrow, the vesper sparrow, and the swamp sparrow. It is a brilliant and charming songster, one of the very finest; but it would be too costly a bargain to buy its presence with loss of the song sparrow's abounding versatility and high spirits, and the vesper sparrow's unfailing sweetness, serenity, and charm.

So much for the sparrows, commonly so called. If we come to the family as a whole, the goodly family of sparrows and finches, we miss in Tennessee the rose-breasted grosbeak and the purple finch, two of our best esteemed Massachusetts birds, both for music and for beauty; to offset which we have the cardinal grosbeak, whose whistle is exquisite, but who can hardly be ranked as a singer above either the rose-breast or the linnet, to say nothing of the two combined.

At the season of my visit, — in the latter half of the vernal migration, — the preponderance of woodland birds, especially of the birds known as wood warblers, was very striking. Of ninety-three species observed, twenty-eight belonged to the warbler family. In this list it was curious to remark the absence of the Nashville and the Tennessee. The circumstance is significant of the comparative worthlessness — except from a historical point of view — of locality names as they are applied to American birds in general. Here were Maryland yellow-throats, Cape May warblers, Canada warblers, Kentucky warblers, prairie warblers, palm warblers, Acadian flycatchers, but not the two birds (the only two, as well as I remember) that bear Tennessee names.[1] The absence of the Nashville was a matter of wonderment to me. Dr. Rives, I have since noticed, records it as only a rare migrant in Virginia. Yet by some route it reaches eastern New England in decidedly handsome numbers. Its congener, the blue golden-wing, surprised me in an opposite direction, — by its commonness, both in the lower

---

[1] Both these warblers — the Nashville and the Tennessee — were named by Wilson from the places where the original specimens were shot. Concerning the Tennessee warbler he sets down the opinion that "it is most probably a native of a more southerly climate." It would be a pity for men to cease guessing, though the shrewdest are certain to be sometimes wrong.

country near the river and on Walden's Ridge. This, too, is a rare bird in Virginia; so much so that Dr. Rives has never met with it there. In certain places about Chattanooga it was as common as it is locally in the towns about Boston, where, to satisfy a skeptical friend, I once counted eleven males in song in the course of a morning's walk. That the Chattanooga birds were on their breeding grounds I had at the time no question, although I happened upon no proof of the fact.

In the same way, from the manner in which the oven-birds were scattered over Walden's Ridge in the middle of May, I assumed, rather hastily, that they were at home for the summer. Months afterward, however, happening to notice their southern breeding limits as given by the best of authorities, — "breeding from . . . Virginia northward," — I saw that I might easily have been in error. I wrote, therefore, to a Chattanooga gentleman, who pays attention to birds while disclaiming acquaintance with ornithology, and he replied that if the oven-bird summered in that country he did not know it. The case seemed to be going

against me, but I bethought myself of Mr.
Brewster's "Ornithological Reconnaissance
in Western North Carolina," and there I
read,[1] "The open oak woodlands, so preva-
lent in this region, are in every way adapted
to the requirements of the oven-bird, and
throughout them it is one of the commonest and most characteristic summer birds."
"Open oak woodlands" is exactly descrip-
tive of the Walden's Ridge forest; and eastern Tennessee and western North Carolina
being practically one, I resume my assured
belief (personal and of no authority) that
the birds I saw and heard were, as I first
thought, natives of the mountain. Birds
which are at home have, as a rule, an air
of being at home; a certain manner hard
to define, but felt, nevertheless, as a pretty
strong kind of evidence — not proof — by a
practiced observer.

Several of the more northern species of
the warbler family manifested an almost ex-
clusive preference for patches of evergreens.
I have elsewhere detailed my experience in
a grove of stunted pines on Lookout Mountain. A similar growth is found on Cam-

---

[1] *The Auk*, vol. iii. p. 175.

eron Hill, — in the city of Chattanooga, — one side of which is occupied by dwellings, while the other drops to the river so precipitously as to be almost inaccessible, and is even yet, I was told, an abode of foxes. On the day after my arrival I strolled to the top of the hill toward evening, and in the pines found a few black-polls and yellow-rumps. I was in a listless mood, having already taken a fair day's exercise under an intolerable sun, but I waked up with a start when my glass fell on a bird which at a second glance showed the red cheeks of a Cape May warbler. For a moment I was almost in poor Susan's case, —

"I looked, and my heart was in heaven."

Then, all too soon, as happened to poor Susan also, the vision faded. But I had seen it. Yes, here it was in Tennessee, the rarity for which, spring after spring, I had been so many years on the watch. I had come South to find it, after all, — a bird that breeds from the northern border of New England to Hudson's Bay !

It is of the nature of such excitements that, at the time, the subject of them has no thought of analyzing or justifying his emotions. He is better employed. Afterward, in some vacant mood, with no longer anything actively to enjoy, he may play with the past, and from an evil habit, or flattering himself with a show of intellectuality, may turn his former delight into a study; tickling his present conceit of himself by smiling at the man he used to be. How very wise he has grown, to be sure! All such refinements, nevertheless, if he did but know it, are only a poorer kind of child's play; less spontaneous, infinitely less satisfying, and equally irrational. Ecstasy is not to be assayed by any test that the reason is competent to apply; nor does it need either defense or apology. It is its own end, and so, like beauty, its own excuse for being. That is one of the crowning felicities of this present order of things, — the world, as we call it. What dog would hunt if there were no excitement in overhauling the game? And how would elderly people live through long evenings if there were no exhilaration in the odd trick?

"What good does it do?" a prudent friend and adviser used to say to me, smiling

at the fervor of my first ornithological en-
thusiasm. He thought he was asking me
a poser; but I answered gayly, " It makes
me happy; " and taking things as they run,
happiness is a pretty substantial "good."
So was it now with the sight of this long-
desired warbler. It taught me nothing; it
put nothing into my pocket; but it made
me happy, — happy enough to sing and
shout, though I am ashamed to say I did
neither. And even a sober son of the Puri-
tans may be glad to find himself, in some
unexpected hour, almost as ineffably delighted as he used to be with a new plaything
in the time when he had not yet tasted of
the tree of knowledge, and knew not that
the relish for playthings could ever be outgrown. I cannot affirm that I went quite
as wild over my first Cape May warbler as
I did over my first sled (how well the rapture
of that frosty midwinter morning is remembered, — a hard crust on the snow, and the
sun not yet risen!), but I came as near to
that state of heavenly felicity — to reënter
which we must become as little children —
as a person of my years is ever likely to do,
perhaps.

It is one precious advantage of natural history studies that they afford endless opportunities for a man to enjoy himself in this sweetly childish spirit, while at the same time his occupation is dignified by a certain scientific atmosphere and relationship. He is a collector of insects, let us say. Whether he goes to the Adirondacks for the summer, or to Florida for the winter, he is surrounded with nets and cyanide bottles. He travels with them as another travels with packs of cards. Every day's catch is part of the game; and once in a while, as happened to me on Cameron Hill, he gets a " great hand," and in imagination, at least, sweeps the board. Commonplace people smile at him, no doubt; but that is only amusing, and he smiles in turn. He can tell many good stories under that head. He delights to be called a " crank." It is all because of people's ignorance. They have no idea that he is Mr. So-and-So, the entomologist; that he is in correspondence with learned men the country over; that he once discovered a new cockroach, and has had a grasshopper named after him; that he has written a book, or is going to write one. Happy man! a contributor to the world's knowledge, but a pleasure-seeker; a little of a savant, and very much of a child; a favorite of Heaven, whose work is play. No wonder it is commonly said that natural historians are a cheerful set.

For the supplying of rarities and surprises there are no birds like the warblers. Their pursuit is the very spice of American ornithology. The multitude of species (Mr. Chapman's "Handbook of the Birds of Eastern North America" enumerates forty-five species and sub-species) is of itself an incalculable blessing in this respect. No single observer is likely ever to come to the end of them. They do not warble, it must be owned, and few of them have much distinction as singers, the best that I know being the black-throated green and the Kentucky; but they are elegant and varied in their plumage, with no lack of bright tints, while their extreme activity and their largely arboreal habits render their specific determination and their individual study a work most agreeably difficult and tantalizing. The ornithologist who has seen all the warblers of his own territory, say of New England, and knows them all by their notes, and has found all their nests, — well, he is himself a pretty rare specimen.

As for my experience with the family in Tennessee, I was glad, of course, to scrape acquaintance — or to renew it, as the case might be — with the more southern species, the Kentucky, the hooded, the cerulean, the blue-wing, and the yellow-throat: that was partly why I was here; but perhaps I enjoyed quite as keenly the sight of our own New England birds moving homeward; tarrying here and there for a day, but not to be tempted by all the allurements of this fine country; still pushing on, northward, and still northward, as if for them there were no place in the world but the woods where they were born. Of the southern species just named, the Kentucky was the most abundant, with the hooded not far behind. The prairie warbler seemed about as common here as in its favored Massachusetts haunts; but unless my ear was at fault its song went somewhat less trippingly: it sounded labored, — too much like the scarlet tanager's in the way of effort and jerkiness. Unlike the golden warbler, the prairie was found not only in the lower country, but —

in less numbers — on Walden's Ridge.   The
two warblers that I listed every day, no
matter where I went, were the chat and the
black-and-white creeper.

When all is said, the Kentucky, with its
beauty and its song, is the star of the family,
as far as eastern Tennessee is concerned.   I
can hear it now, while Falling Water goes
babbling past in the shade of laurel and
rhododendron.   As for the chat, it was om-
nipresent: in the valley, along the river, on
Missionary Ridge, on Lookout Mountain,
on Walden's Ridge, in the national cemetery,
at Chickamauga, — everywhere, in short,
except within the city itself.   In this regard
it exceeded the white-eyed vireo, and even
the indigo-bird, I think.   Black-polls were
seen daily up to May 13, after which they
were missing altogether.   The last Cape
May and the last yellow-rump were noted on
the 8th, the last redstart and the last palm
warbler on the 11th, the last chestnut-side,
magnolia, and Canadian warbler on the 12th.
On the 12th, also, I saw my only Wilson's
black-cap.   In my last outing, on the 18th,
on Walden's Ridge, I came upon two Black-
burnians in widely separate places.   At the

time, I assumed them to be migrants, in spite
of the date. One of them was near the
hotel, on ground over which I had passed
almost daily. Why they should be so be-
hindhand was more than I could tell; but
only the day before I had seen a thrush
which was either a gray-cheek or an olive-
back, and of course a bird of passage. "The
flight of warblers did not pass entirely until
May 19," says Mr. Jeffries, writing of what
he saw in western North Carolina.[1]

The length of time occupied by some
species in accomplishing their semi-annual
migration is well known to be very considerable, and is best observed — in spring, at
least — at some southern point. It is admir-
ably illustrated in Mr. Chapman's " List of
Birds seen at Gainesville, Florida."[2] Tree
swallows, he tells us, were abundant up to
May 6, a date at which Massachusetts tree
swallows have been at home for nearly or
quite a month. Song sparrows were noted
March 31, two or three weeks after the
grand irruption of song sparrows into
Massachusetts usually occurs. Bobolinks,

[1] *The Auk*, vol. vi. p. 120.
[2] *Ibid.*, vol. v. p. 267.

which reach Massachusetts by the 10th of
May, or earlier, were still very abundant —
both sexes — May 25! Such dates are not
what we should have expected, I suppose,
especially in the case of a bird like the
bobolink, which has no very high northern
range ; but they seem not to be exceptional,
and are surprising only because we have not
yet mastered the general subject. Nothing
exists by itself, and therefore nothing can
be understood by itself. One thing the
most ignorant of us may see, — that the
long period covered by the migratory jour-
neys is a matter for ornithological thankfulness. In Massachusetts, for example, spring
migrants begin to appear in late February
or early March, and some of the most interesting members of the procession — notably
the mourning warbler and the yellow-bellied
flycatcher — are to be looked for after the
first of June. The autumnal movement is
equally protracted ; so that for at least half
the year — leaving winter with its arctic
possibilities out of consideration — we may
be on the lookout for strangers.

One of the dearest pleasures of a southern
trip in winter or early spring is the very

thing at which I have just now hinted, the sight of one's home birds in strange surroundings. You leave New England in early February, for instance, and in two or three days are loitering in the sunny pinelands about St. Augustine, with the trees full of robins, bluebirds, and pine warblers, and the savanna patches full of meadow larks. Myrtle warblers are everywhere. Phœbes salute you as you walk the city streets, and flocks of chippers and vesper sparrows enliven the fields along the country roads. In a piece of hammock just outside the town you find yourself all at once surrounded by a winter colony of summer birds. Here are solitary vireos, Maryland yellow-throats, black-and-white creepers, prairie warblers, red-poll warblers, hermit thrushes, red-eyed chewinks, thrashers, catbirds, cedar-birds, and many more. White-eyed vireos are practicing in the smilax thickets, — though they have small need of practice, — and white-bellied swallows go flashing and twittering overhead. The world is good, you say, and life is a festival.

My vacation in Tennessee afforded less of contrast and surprise, for a twofold reason :

it was near the end of April, instead of early
in February, so that migrants had been arriving in Massachusetts for six or seven weeks
before my departure; and Tennessee has nothing of the foreign, half-tropical look which
Florida presents to Yankee eyes; but even
so, it was no small pleasure to step suddenly into a world full of summer music.
Such multitudes of birds as were singing
on Missionary Ridge on that first bright
forenoon! The number of species was not
great, when it came to counting them, —
morning and afternoon together yielded but
forty-two; but the whole country seemed
alive with wings. And of the forty-two
species, thirty-two were such as summer in
Massachusetts or pass through it to their
homes beyond. Here were already (April
27) the olive-backed thrush, and northern
warblers like the black-poll, the bay-breast,
and the Cape May, none of which would be
due in Massachusetts for at least a fortnight.
Here, too, were yellow-rumps and white-
throated sparrows, though the advance
guard of both species had reached New England before I left home. The white-throats
lingered on Walden's Ridge on the 13th of

May, a fact which surprised me more at the time than it does in the review.

One bird was seen on this first day, and not afterward. I had been into the woods north of the city, and was returning, when from the bridge over the Tennessee I caught sight of a small flock of black birds, which at first, even with the aid of my glass, I could not make out, the bridge being so high above the river and its banks. While I was watching them, however, they began to sing. They were bobolinks. Probably the species is not common in eastern Tennessee, as the name is wanting in Dr. Fox's "List of Birds found in Roane County, Tennessee, during April, 1884, and March and April, 1885." [1]

I have ventured upon some slight ornithological comparison between southeastern Tennessee and eastern Massachusetts, and, writing as a patriot (or a partisan), have

[1] *The Auk*, vol. iii. p. 315. Of sixty-two species seen by me during the last four days of April, eleven are not given by Dr. Fox, namely, Wilson's thrush, black-poll warbler, bay-breasted warbler, Cape May warbler, black-throated blue warbler, palm warbler, chestnut-sided warbler, blue golden-winged warbler, bobolink, Acadian flycatcher, yellow-billed cuckoo.

seen to it that the scale inclined northward.
To this end I have made as much as possible
of the absence of robins, song sparrows, and
vesper sparrows, and of the comparative
dearth of swallows; but of course the loyal
Tennessean is in no want of a ready answer.
Robins, song sparrows, vesper sparrows, and
swallows are *not* absent, except as breeding
birds. He has them all in their season,[1]
and probably hears them sing. On the
whole, then, he may fairly retort, he has
considerably the advantage of us Yankees:
he sees our birds on their passage, and
drinks his fill of their music before we have
caught the first spring notes; while we, on
the other hand, see nothing of his distinc-
tively southern birds unless we come South
for the purpose. Well, they are worth the
journey. Bachman's finch alone — yes, the
one dingy, shabbily clad little genius by
the Chickamauga well — might almost have
repaid me for my thousand miles on the rail.

It was a strange mingling of sensations
that possessed me in Chattanooga. The
city itself was like other cities of its age

[1] See Dr. Fox's list.

and size, with some appearance of a community that had been in haste to grow, — a
trifle impatient, shall we say (impatience
being one of the virtues of youth), to pull
down its barns and build greater; just now
a little checked in its ambition, as things
looked; yet still enterprising, still fairly
well satisfied with itself, with no lack of
energy and bustle. As it happened, there
was a stir in local politics at the time of my
visit (possibly there always is), and at the
street corners all patriotic citizens were ex-
horted to do their duty. " Vote for Tom
—— for sheriff," said one placard. " Vote
for Bob ——," said another, in capitals
equally importunate. In Tennessee, as
everywhere else, the politician knows his
trade. Familiarity, readiness with the hand,
freedom with one's own name (Tom, not
Thomas, if you please), and a happy knack
at remembering the names of other people,
— these are some of the preëlection tests of
statesmanship.

All in all, then, between politics and
business, the city was " very much alive," as
the saying goes; but somehow it was not so
often the people about me that occupied my

thoughts as those who had been here thirty
years before. Precious is the power of a
first impression. Because I was newly in
the country I was constantly under the feeling of its past. Hither and thither I went
in the region round about, listening at every
turn, spying into every bush at the stirring
of a leaf or the chirp of a bird ; yet I had
always with me the men of '63, and felt
always that I was on holy ground.

A LIST OF BIRDS

Found in the Neighborhood of Chattanooga
from April 27 to May 18, 1894.

1. Green Heron. *Ardea virescens.* — A single individual seen from a car window. No other water birds were observed except three or four ducks and a single wader, all upon the wing and unidentified.

2. Bob White. Quail. Partridge. *Colinus virginianus.* — Common.

3. Ruffed Grouse. "Pheasant." *Bonasa umbellus.* — Heard drumming on Walden's Ridge.

4. Carolina Dove. Mourning Dove. *Zenaidura macroura.* — A small number seen.

5. Turkey Vulture. Turkey Buzzard. *Cathartes aura.* — Common.

6. Black Vulture. Carrion Crow. *Catharista atrata.* — Two birds seen.

7. Red-tailed Hawk. *Buteo borealis* — One bird seen from Walden's Ridge.

8. Sparrow Hawk. *Falco sparverius.* — One bird, on Walden's Ridge.

9. Yellow - billed Cuckoo. *Coccyzus americanus.* — Common. First noticed April 29.

10. Black-billed Cuckoo. *Coccyzus erythrophthalmus.* — Seen twice on Lookout Mountain, May 7 and 8, and once on Walden's Ridge, May 12.

11. Belted Kingfisher. *Ceryle alcyon.* — A single bird heard on Walden's Ridge.

12. Hairy Woodpecker. *Dryobates villosus.* — My notes record seven birds. No attempt was made to determine

their specific or sub-specific identity, but they are pre-
sumed to have been *D. villosus*, not *D. villosus audubonii.*

13. Downy Woodpecker.   *Dryobates pubescens.* — **A**
single bird was heard (not seen) on Walden's Ridge, — a
noticeable reversal of the usual relative commonness of
this species and the preceding.

14. Red-cockaded Woodpecker.   *Dryobates borealis.* —
Found only at Chickamauga, on Snodgrass Hill, in long-
leaved pines — two or three birds.

15. Pileated Woodpecker.   "Logcock."   *Ceophlœus
pileatus.* — Said to be common on Walden's Ridge, where
I heard its flicker-like shout.

16. Red-headed Woodpecker.   *Melanerpes erythrocepha-
lus.* — One seen near Missionary Ridge and one at Chickamauga.   The scarcity of this bird, and the absence of
the red-bellied and the yellow-bellied, were among the
surprises of my visit.

17. Flicker.   Golden-winged Woodpecker.   *Colaptes
auratus.* — Not common.   Three birds were seen at Chickamauga, and it was occasional on Walden's Ridge, where
I listed it five days of the seven.

18. Whippoorwill.   *Antrostomus vociferus.* — Un-
doubtedly common.   I heard it only on Walden's Ridge,
the only place where I went into the woods after dark.

19. Nighthawk.   *Chordeiles virginianus.* — Common.

20. Chimney Swift.   *Chætura pelagica.* — Abundant.

21. Ruby-throated Humming-bird.   *Trochilus colubris.*
— Common in the forests of Walden's Ridge.   Seen but
twice elsewhere.   First seen April 28.

22. Kingbird.   *Tyrannus tyrannus.* — Seen but **three**
times — nine specimens in all.   First seen April 29.

23. Crested Flycatcher.   *Myiarchus crinitus.* — Noticed
daily, with two exceptions.

24. Phœbe.   *Sayornis phœbe.* — Common on Lookout
Mountain and Walden's Ridge.   Not seen elsewhere.

25. Wood Pewee. *Contopus virens.* — Very common. Much the most numerous member of the family. Present in good force April 27, and gathering nest materials April 29.

26. Acadian Flycatcher. Green-crested Flycatcher. *Empidonax virescens.* — Common.

27. Blue Jay. *Cyanocitta cristata.* — Scarce (for the blue jay), and not seen on Walden's Ridge!

28. Crow. *Corvus americanus.* — Apparently much less common than in Eastern Massachusetts.

29. Bobolink. *Dolichonyx oryzivorus.* — A small flock seen, and heard singing, April 27.

30. Orchard Oriole. *Icterus spurius.* — Common, but not found on Walden's Ridge.

31. Baltimore Oriole. *Icterus galbula.* — A single bird, at Chickamauga, May 3.

32. Crow Blackbird. *Quiscalus quiscula ?* — Seen on sundry occasions in the valley country, but specific distinction not made out. Both forms — *Q. quiscula* and *Q. quiscula œneus* — are found in Tennessee. See Dr. Fox's List of Birds found in Roane County, Tennessee. "The Auk," vol. iii. p. 315. My own list of the Icteridæ is remarkable for its omissions, especially of the cowbird, the red-winged blackbird (which, however, I am pretty certain that I saw on the wing) and the meadow lark.

33. House Sparrow. English Sparrow. *Passer domesticus.* — Distressingly superabundant in the city and its suburbs.

34. Goldfinch. *Spinus tristis.* — Abundant. Still in flocks.

35. White-crowned Sparrow. *Zonotrichia leucophrys.* — Seen but once (May 1), two birds, in the national cemetery.

36. White-throated Sparrow. *Zonotrichia albicollis.* — Common. Still present on Walden's Ridge (in two places) May 13. Sang very little.

37. Chipping Sparrow. Doorstep Sparrow. *Spizella socialis.* — Common.

38. Field Sparrow. *Spizella pusilla.* — Common.

39. Bachman's Sparrow. *Peucœa œstivalis bachmanii.* — Common. One of the best of singers.

40. Chewink. Towhee. *Pipilo erythrophthalmus.* — Rather common. Much less numerous than I should have expected from the nature of the country.

41. Cardinal Grosbeak. *Cardinalis cardinalis.* — Seen daily, but seemingly not very numerous.

42. Rose-breasted Grosbeak. *Habia ludoviciana.* — A single female, May 11.

43. Indigo-bird. *Passerina cyanea.* — Very abundant. For the first time I saw this tropical-looking beauty in flocks.

44. Scarlet Tanager. *Piranga erythromelas.* — Common on the mountains, but seemingly rare in the valley.

45. Summer Tanager. *Piranga rubra.* — Common throughout.

46. Purple Martin. *Progne subis.* — Common.

47. Rough-winged Swallow. *Stelgidopteryx serripennis.* — A few birds seen.

48. Red-eyed Vireo. *Vireo olivaceus.* — Common. One of the species listed every day.

49. Yellow-throated Vireo. *Vireo flavifrons.* — Common. Seen or heard every day except April 27.

50. White-eyed Vireo. *Vireo noveboracensis.* — Abundant. Heard every day.

51. Black - and - white Creeper. *Mniotilta varia.* — Very common.

52. Blue-winged Warbler. *Helminthophila pinus.* — One bird seen at Chickamauga, and a pair on Missionary Ridge.

53. Golden-winged Warbler. *Helminthophila chrysoptera.* — Common, especially in the broken woods north of the city.

54. Parula Warbler. Blue Yellow-backed Warbler. *Compsothlypis americana.* — Only on Walden's Ridge.

55. Cape May Warbler. *Dendroica tigrina.* — One bird seen on Cameron Hill, and a small company on Lookout Mountain — April 27, and May 7 and 8.

56. Yellow Warbler. Golden Warbler. *Dendroica æstiva.* — Common, but not observed on Walden's Ridge.

57. Black-throated Blue Warbler. *Dendroica cærulescens.* — Common, April 27 to May 14.

58. Myrtle Warbler. Yellow-rumped Warbler. *Dendroica coronata.* — Noted April 27 and 28, and May 7 and 8.

59. Magnolia Warbler. *Dendroica maculosa.* — Not uncommon, May 1 to 12.

60. Cerulean Warbler. *Dendroica cærulea.* — One bird, a male in song, on Lookout Mountain.

61. Chestnut-sided Warbler. *Dendroica pensylvanica.* — Listed on six dates — April 27 to May 12.

62. Bay - breasted Warbler. *Dendroica castanea.* — Seven or eight individuals — April 27 to May 10.

63. Black-poll Warbler. *Dendroica striata.* — Common to May 13.

64. Blackburnian Warbler. *Dendroica blackburniæ.* — Seven birds — May 1 to 18.

65. Yellow - throated Warbler. *Dendroica dominica.* (*Albilora ?*) — Found only at Chickamauga (Snodgrass Hill), where it seemed to be common.

66. Black-throated green Warbler. *Dendroica virens.* — Common.

67. Pine Warbler. *Dendroica vigorsii.* — Not numerous, but found in appropriate places.

68. Palm Warbler. *Dendroica palmarum.* — The specific — or sub-specific — identity of this bird was not certainly determined, but I judged the specimens — seen on four dates, April 29 to May 11 — to be as above given, rather than *D. palmarum hypochrysea.*

69. Prairie Warbler. *Dendroica discolor.* — Very common.

70. Oven-bird. *Seiurus aurocapillus.* — Common on Lookout Mountain and Walden's Ridge. Seen but once in the lower country.

71. Louisiana Water-thrush. *Seiurus motacilla.* — A few birds seen on Walden's Ridge.

72. Kentucky Warbler. *Geothlypis formosa.* — Very common, and in places very unlike.

73. Maryland Yellow - throat. *Geothlypis trichas.* — Common.

74. Yellow-breasted Chat. *Icteria virens.* — Very common.

75. Hooded Warbler. *Sylvania mitrata.* — Common, especially along the woodland streams on Walden's Ridge.

76. Wilson's Blackcap. *Sylvania pusilla.* — A single bird on Walden's Ridge, May 12, in free song.

77. Canadian Warbler. *Sylvania canadensis.* — Seen on three dates — May 6, 11, and 12.

78. Redstart. *Setophaga ruticilla.* — Common. Not seen after May 14.

79. Mocking-bird. *Mimus polyglottos.* — Rare. Not found on the mountains.

80. Catbird. *Galeoscoptes carolinensis.* — Very common, both in the city and in the country round about.

81. Brown Thrasher. *Harporhynchus rufus.* — Common.

82. Carolina Wren. Mocking Wren. *Thryothorus ludovicianus.* — Common.

83. Bewick's Wren. *Thryothorus bewickii.* — Not common. Seen only on Missionary Ridge.

84. White-breasted Nuthatch. *Sitta carolinensis.* — Common at Chickamauga and on Walden's Ridge. A single bird noticed on Lookout Mountain.

85. Tufted Titmouse. *Parus bicolor.* — Common.

86. Carolina Chickadee. *Parus carolinensis.* — Common.

87. Blue - gray Gnatcatcher. *Polioptila cærulea.* — Common.

88. Wood Thrush. *Turdus mustelinus.* — Very common. A bird with its beak full of nest materials was seen April 29, at the base of Missionary Ridge.

89. Wilson's Thrush. Veery. *Turdus fuscescens.* — Rare.

90. Gray-cheeked Thrush. *Turdus aliciæ,* or *T. aliciæ bicknelli.* — Two birds, May 2 and 13.

91. Swainson's Thrush. Olive-backed Thrush. *Turdus ustulatus swainsonii.* — In good numbers and free song. Seen on four dates, the latest being May 12.

92. Robin. *Merula migratoria.* — Five birds in the national cemetery, April 29.

93. Bluebird. *Sialia sialis.* — Common. Young birds out of the nest, April 28.

INDEX.